THE WIND RIDERS

Wirrun's hand closed on the Power. Its strength flowed into him, and he held out the loop of cord from it to the stick-thin rock-spirit beside him. He and the Mimi walked into daylight with the wind in their faces. Whenever it strengthened, the Mimi tensed and gripped the cord anxiously. Wind was a great terror for her, yet she faced it without faltering.

She began a long-legged lope. He had to race to keep beside her. Then wind curled around him and swung him up, with the Mimi bobbing on the cord above him. When he opened his eyes, they were high above the trees with the old land brooding darkly below.

"THIS IS STRONG AND ORIGINAL FANTASY BY A RE-MARKABLE STORYTELLER. MS. WRIGHTSON'S WRIT-ING HAS THE EVOCATIVE POWER OF THE FIRST THINGS AND THE GREAT ONES OF THE LAND; AND HER VIVID SENSE OF HER CHARACTERS MAKES THEIR ADVENTURES BOTH GRIPPING AND POIGNANT."

—Stephen R. Donaldson
Author of *The Chronicles of Thomas Covenant*

THE ICE
IS COMING

❖❖❖❖❖❖❖❖❖❖❖❖❖❖❖❖❖❖❖❖❖❖❖❖❖❖❖❖❖❖❖❖❖❖❖❖❖❖

Patricia Wrightson

A Del Rey Book

BALLANTINE BOOKS • NEW YORK

A Del Rey Book
Published by Ballantine Books

Copyright © 1977 by Patricia Wrightson

Library of Congress Catalog Card Number: 76-45438

ISBN 0-345-29485-8

This edition published by arrangement with
Atheneum Publishers

Manufactured in the United States of America

First Ballantine Books Edition: November 1981

Cover art by Michael Whelan

Contents

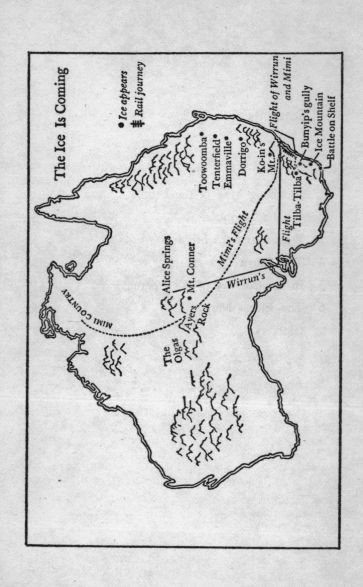

The Ice Is Coming

● Ice appears
╪ Rail journey

Toowoomba *
Tenterfield *
Emmaville *
Dorrigo *
Ko-in's Mt. *
Flight of Wirrun and Mimi
Bunyip's gully
Ice Mountain
Battle on Shelf
Flight
Tilba-Tilba *

Mimi's Flight

Alice Springs
Mt. Conner
Wirrun's
Ayers Rock

MIMI COUNTRY

The Olgas

Author's Note

This is a story of today and of Australia. It is my own story, grown out of my thinking. Its human characters are my invention, but its spirit characters are not. They are the folk-spirits of the Australian Aborigines— not the ritual figures of the creative myths but the gnomes and heroes and monsters of Australia.

I might have written a story about more familiar spirits, the elves and fairies and dragons and monsters of Europe. Then everyone would have known that the story was mine and the spirits borrowed from an older convention. But for that story I would have to invent a foreign setting, an Earthsea or a Middle Earth; and powerfully magical as those countries are I know one as powerful and as magic. It is the only one I know and the one I want to write about.

So every spirit appearing in this and my two previous stories, *The Nargun and the Stars* and *An Older Kind of Magic*, belongs originally to Australia and its Aborigines. Many of them are beliefs still living; some are remembered from only a generation ago; a few have outlived the people who believed in them. They claim their place in an old convention, these even older and perhaps purer spirits of the Aborigines' domestic life. And I claim a writer's leave to employ them in my own stories in my own way.

1

❖❖

A Young Man
of the People

One

The old south land lies across the world like an open hand, hollowed a little at the palm. High over it tumbles the wind, and all along its margin tumbles the sea—rolling in slow sweeps on long white beaches, beating with hammers of water at headlands of rock. Under and in this tumbling of wind and water the land lies quiet like a great hand at rest, all its power unknown.

Along its green margins, clustered in towns here and there, live the Happy Folk with their faces to the sea. They live for happiness; it is their business and their duty. They study it and teach it to their children, debate it, make laws to force it on each other, struggle for it, export and import it. Most of all they buy and sell it. They have no time to look over their shoulders at the old land behind them. Only sometimes, in their search for happiness, they make expensive little explorations into the land with cameras.

The Happy Folk know that they are the land's true people and everything in it belongs to them. Yet between the towns, and inland behind cliffed and chasmed mountains, live other races. There are only a few of them, thinly scattered: the Inlanders and the People. The People are dark-skinned, with heavy brows and watching eyes, and they belong to the land; it flows into them through their feet. The time when they took the land from another people is so long ago that they can forget it and claim the land as theirs; but really it is the land that claims them.

The Inlanders come from the same stock as the Happy Folk, and the two still claim to be of the same race. But the great old silent land that claims the People for its own has been at work on the Inlanders too, and by now they have become a separate race. The Inlanders suspect it with bitterness, the Happy Folk laugh and deny it. Between the Inlanders and the People there is another sort of bitterness: they are both jealous children of the land.

So these races struggle to come together and drift farther apart, while the oldest race of all lives among them and is hidden. This is a race of creatures born of the land itself: of red rocks and secret waters, dust-devils and far places, green jungle and copper-blue salt-bush. They are sly and secret creatures. The People have known of them for a long time and said little. As for the other two races, if a man of them ever meets an earth-spirit he is silent for lack of a word and so no word is said.

Among the oldest of all are the Narguns, monsters of rock poured molten from the fires in the heart of the land. Far down the world they live, near the south-east corner of the land, crouched in the darkness of caves or holes in the ground. Long before the white races came to the land the People had learnt to avoid those caves in case death should roll out of them, quick and crushing. If Narguns are old, the Eldest Nargun is as old as the land itself; and because it is the oldest, and closest to the heart of the land, the red fire of its beginning will come when it calls.

For thousands of years the Eldest Nargun lay in the dark of the earth. In time it emerged, the first, the biggest and most powerful. It felt starlight and wind and saw great battles; and when those were over it found a cave and went into darkness again. In later times it took its power into battle against the sea, standing against the sea where it tears at the edge of the land.

The Nargun soon found that the power of fire was useless here. It only stood against the sea as the rocks did. On a rising tide great glassy swells rolled in, exploding in rockets of water or spilling over in sudden flowers of foam. When the tide drew back it left quiet pools where weeds swayed, anemones flowered, and small things made slow journeys from side to side; but still the sea curled long exploring fingers into channels, and sent its puppy-waves licking among the rocks. Sometimes the Nargun lay just covered by water; looking up, the old stone monster saw a rippled sun or washed and wavering stars. Sometimes when deep green swells rolled over, in the tug of water the Eldest moved a little and cried out with its old cry: '*Nga-a-a!*' And there it crouches still, defying the sea.

Far to the north live the Mimi, and no one knows how old they are. Even the People cannot see them, but they have always known they are there. They know by the paintings in the caves.

In that north country the rough cave walls are crowded with the paintings of the People: paintings of late times and long-ago times and the Dreamtime. All the lore and history of the People are painted on the walls of those caves, and the People look and know and remember. But among those paintings there are some that were not made by the People. They are no part of the People's lore, so they know that those paintings were made by the Mimi. From the paintings they have learnt much about the Mimi themselves.

The Mimi are shy spirits who live inside the rocks. When they blow on a rock it opens to let them in or out. They have very sharp eyes and ears; at the first sign of a stranger they slip away into their rocks, and this is why the People never see them.

Their paintings show that they hunt with spear and spear-thrower in the normal way, and dig with digging sticks and cook with fire. They are very tall and thin and frail, so frail that the wind might break them. Because of this they never gather food in windy weather but only when it is calm. But once there was a Mimi who was caught by the wind and carried far away; and perhaps it was the old south land itself that called up that wind.

It was late spring: the time when the trade winds tramp south, when in the north stray winds play to and fro, soft and hard, till the monsoons come down. These uncertain winds had kept this Mimi inside her rock until her food was running short. In the first calm she went out with her digging stick and her bark dish to dig roots and honey-ants in a place near at hand.

She heard the first hissing of leaves in the wind, but her digging stick had caught under a root. She waited only a second to jerk it free, snatched up her basket, and sprang like a spider to a rock. She blew to open it—but the tricky spring wind swirled along the rock and blew her breath away. Then it tugged her legs into the air. Her body strained at the weight of basket and stick—she dropped them quickly in case she should break. So the updraught caught her like a straw, and the wind had her.

'*Wa!*' she cried thinly, whirling and spinning. She twisted her arms and legs together to keep them from being torn off. The wind spun her upward and swung her south in a wide curve.

Tumbling in waves of wind she caught glimpses of her country below: stooping rocks and shadowed gorges and flat green swamps, all the dear known country spinning in corroboree. She was still reaching for it when her country danced north and away.

Strange winds dropped and caught her, passed her from one to another and carried her higher, and still she did not break. She was learning to hold her wispy arms and legs together and to lie along the wind. She came swooping down: a black speck below grew into a grey tree-top that she tried to catch before she was whirled up again. She saw a tide of darkness creep over the land and night come. The stars swung to and fro, and she wondered with terror how she should get back to her country. Already the wind had carried her down the old south land to its beautiful, terrible heart; and there, though she did not know it, something waited.

The centre of the old south land is a place of waiting; of waiting and of age. In the palm of that great hand lies the age and travail of the world, and the Happy Folk call it a desert. Here the ground lies so level that water will not flow, and empty river-courses lead only into clay pans crusted with salt. The sun beats down like a gong on red wind-drifted dunes. Flat-topped mountains, painted red with sand, are not mountains at all but single, enduring, rocks quarried by winds and seas far off in time. Desert creatures hide by day under spinifex and saltbush and slow brave mulga. And under the castle-ramparts of a mountain lies one small lake of dried salt, where one small outcrop of rock leads down to the caverns of the Ninya.

Under the fiery sand they live, men of ice in caverns of ice. No icicles drip from their cavern roofs, for there is never any melting here. There is only the whiteness of frost never touched, and a shining floor of ice, and columns and arches of ice that the Ninya build for pleasure, and a frozen howling wind. The Ninya are men like men of the People, except that they like their caverns are pure and sparkling white. Their eyebrows and beards are needles of ice, and frost falls from them as they move. Wherever they go through the caverns, the frost and ice and the cold wind go with them. They are the makers of ice and their blood is white.

They are green-eyed and beautiful and they live together as brothers, but there is no kindness between them. The frost goes deep. Their voices creak and grate; they often howl in anger; and every man of the Ninya wants all and wants it for himself. So this power of wanting and this power of ice lie under the sun-beaten sand, prisoned and waiting.

On that day when the spring wind caught the Mimi, the waiting had exploded into quarrels. The cold white vaults were beautiful, but it was always twilight there and the sparkle of frost was dim. The Ninya yearned over that. The wind's howl should have widened into a song; it needed a sky. The ice wanted sun to touch it to green and blue fire; they longed to see it. Bitterly they snarled at each other.

'*You* may hide like a black bat in a cave. I—I will go out and take the land.'

'Go, then—and melt. I wait till the Nargun is found.'

'You will crawl out when the ice is built and the frost laid.'

'And without me when will that be? We are few since the days of the Nargun, and all are needed. A frost or two, a little ice to cut the People's feet, and you will melt.'

This sneer brought howls of anger. 'Hear the Great Glacier! He says we are lost without him!' 'The People are gone and we are free, yet he sulks in a cave while the sun burns the land!' But some drew apart from the others and muttered and creaked together.

'We wait till the Nargun is found,' they said at last.

'The Nargun! What is a Nargun? A beast of rock!' 'Can we not freeze rock? Look there!' One of them struck the cavern wall and showered frost into the wind.

'Freeze your own ears—you talk like a fool!' 'We say not a Nargun but *the* Nargun. The Eldest with the power of fire.' 'The one that melted our bones into rivers and sent us under the ground. That Nargun.' 'They have forgotten. They are men without ears.'

There were more howls at the insult, and frosty hands groped for frosty stones. A stronger voice than the others grated through the howl of the wind.

'Stop, you fools! No man can be spared. We are few enough for the work we have to do. You howl for freedom, but when the work begins you waste yourselves in fighting.'

The howls died into mutters. The stones dropped. The Ninya waited to hear how the work might be beginning. The strong-voiced one told them quickly, before the fight could start again.

'Some of you say, go now. Some of you say, first find the Eldest Nargun. I say, go now to find the Eldest Nargun.'

They listened. He went on.

'How shall we find the Nargun? By hiding in a cave? It lies in its own country by the far-off sea. We must go there: a long journey in the winding roads of rock. We must find the Eldest and catch it quickly in a fist of ice. *Then* we are free.'

Creaks of argument broke out, but the voice cut through them quickly and began to chant.

'We will build mountains of ice with the rainbow in them. We will sparkle the ground with frost and feather the air with snow, with the silent feathers of snow.'

'Snow!' they all groaned, for they had not seen it for an age.

'Drill into rocks with the delicate needle of cold; fling a net to trap birds from the air and furry things from the forest. Bind up the running waters and hold them still.'

Now all the Ninya howled and sang together. Frost showered from their swaying bodies and needles of ice from their beards. The first singer listened with a cold white smile and sang a new line.

'In a mountain of ice shall the Nargun, the Eldest, be held.'

But this tore the chorus apart into separate howls. 'We build here, we build now, while the People forget!' 'Why should we journey? Let the Eldest wait by the far-off sea while we grow mighty!' 'As we were before, when the Nargun melted our bones! Find the Nargun, find the Nargun!' 'And who will find it?' 'The ice! The ice will find it!'

Soon the two sides had fallen apart again and instead of singing there were bitter snarls. The wind raged on through the glitter of ice and circled by deeper caverns far into the earth. Above, the sun burnt down on the lake of salt. The surface rock, the Ninya's entrance, baked in the heat.

The sun sank. The land gave back its heat to the shining, paling sky. Flat-topped Mount Conner rose like a castle, sharp against the western sky. Its haze, that most lovely and tender haze of the central hills, was lit to lilac and gold. Acacia blossom rippled with gold in the last breath of falling wind, and brittle-dead flowers chattered in the feathers of an emu-bush. Under a native plum beside the lake, a young man of the People unrolled his sleeping-bag for the night.

Although he was one of the People, this young man was a stranger. He lived among the Happy Folk in the east, because there by the sea was his own country. Until lately he had gone to one of the Happy Folk's schools, and now that that was finished he worked in one of their service stations. He knew the Happy Folk well, and liked to watch and think about them, for he was a young man to whom thinking came more easily than talking. He talked only to his friends.

His friends were among the People of the east who lived as he did, and some he had met as he went up and down the country. A few of his friends called him Wirrun, though he had another name among strangers. He talked to them mostly about the land and the People.

Wirrun didn't know that the land flowed into him through his feet. He only knew that he liked to walk on the earth in lonely places. He spent holidays and weekends doing this; and he had learnt from the Happy Folk the trick of saving money to buy easy travel over long distances. One of his friends in the east had come from the great quiet centre of the land. He often talked about it, and Wirrun listened, and wished he might walk on the red sand. At last he saved up a great amount of money, enough for the plane fare, so that his short holiday would be long enough. And when he had travelled over the wide land as far as that fare would take him he talked to People, asked questions, bought a bus ticket, and explored even further on his feet. So now he unrolled his sleeping-bag beside the small salt lake with its outcrop of rock, and hung his canvas water-bag from a branch of the native plum, and camped there for that night.

Darkness came in a soft sweep, with the lemon-sharp twinkle of stars. Like a spider-web dropped by the wind came the Mimi, slipping down between stars and spinifex. She drifted over the salt scab of the lake, saw the rock and reached for it. She blew on the Ninya's rock and slipped inside.

The night drew on a little and grew chill. Under the wild plum Wirrun slept soundly. A round-eyed mulgara whiffled at his sleeping-bag, then veered off after the scent of a mouse. An orb-spider's golden web shook and swayed to the flapping of a giant moth.

There was a snarling struggle in the lake: a man of the Ninya had burst out through the rock. Starlight sparkled on white arms that fought angrily to drag him back. He was pulled in, and the rock shut solid; and outside, spilt on the salty crust, lay the Mimi. She was frozen stiff with cold and terror.

So they lay that night as the old south land had ordered it: the young man from the east sleeping under the plum, the rock-spirit of the north frozen on the salt. In caverns beneath them the Ninya raged and fought for possession of the land; and far down the world the Eldest Nargun crouched on its shelf of rock while the sea swirled over.

Two

By the small salt lake the chill night had grown suddenly colder, for a gush of cold had come forth with the Ninya. The young man burrowed deeper into his bag, the moth stopped flapping in the web. The Mimi lay stiff for a long time; but presently she wove herself into the spinifex and curled up, shivering.

She was far and far from home, in an unknown country whose wandering night-things might find her and be angry. She had never lain before under the prickling stars, and she longed for the soft utter blackness of rock. Yet this rock here had been a trap; her poor wispy wits were in a tangle. What she had seen and

heard in the rock had chilled her with fear as well as
cold. It reached back into the past, to some old dread
that she couldn't remember and couldn't forget.

She lay all night, a long loop in the spinifex, watching with frightened eyes round and dark like a possum's
and listening with her large ears. She saw and heard the
mulgara eating the mouse, the moth hanging in the
web, and the young man of the People sleeping. She
saw daylight begin to flow in slow waves from the east,
but when it was newly shining she pressed her hands
over her eyes and whimpered softly. Not this—she
couldn't look at this—

Wirrun woke and sat up to look at the country. Like
the Mimi he shut his eyes again quickly. He opened
them, stared at the ground beside him, then slowly
raised his eyes and looked again.

Yes. The country was hanging upside down and
floating in the air.

Salt lake and emu-bush, mulga and red sand and the
distant castle-mountain of Conner, all of it floated the
wrong way up. Trees and bushes reached down with
grey leaves, trying to get back. There was a shimmer at
the edges of it, like cellophane. If last night's wind came
back now and blew it away . . .?

A quietness came over him and told him not to look
because this was not his country. In a moment, surely,
it would put itself right for strangers. Because he had
been to school and learnt about mirages he knew this
must be something of that kind—but he didn't want to
look at it.

He turned away to wait, and reached for his water-
bag hanging on the branch above him. The bag crackled under his hand, and a thin glassy coating slid from
it down to his shoulder. He shook it off hard. This time
it was the shock of cold that startled him. He saw that
now the floating upside-down country had slipped back
into place. The great gold gong of the sun beat down on
the saltbush. It was late October—almost summer; and
there was ice on his water-bag.

He remembered again that he was a stranger here.

'You'll get funny weather any time,' said Wirrun politely, rubbing the unshaved hair on his round young chin.

He breakfasted, rolled his gear neatly and slung it from his shoulder, took down his water-bag, and walked away from the small salt lake under Mount Conner. He didn't know that the Mimi watched him from the spinifex; he had to reach the road in time to catch a bus. As he walked he looked, far and near. He could not afford a camera as well as a plane fare; he had to trust his eyes and mind.

He saw a flight of green parrots, and the sand glowing red between the saltbush, and the brilliant blue of a small strange flower. He must ask someone about that. He saw the sharp, clear lines of sandhill and mountain against the sky—but this he knew was a pretence because from the plane he had seen the truth. This country had no horizon. From above you could see it spreading out and out till it melted and vanished in purple haze. There was no true meeting of land and sky, no horizon.

A country with no horizon . . . could it come loose and float in the air? And ice in October. . . . What could the People of this country tell him? If they would?

He reached the road and heard the bus: first a tingle in the ears, then a whisper, then a whine, and at last a moaning motor. It stopped at his signal. He found a seat at the back and watched the Happy Folk returning from exploration, their cameras full of happiness. They were building little webs of friendship meant to last a day or so. Wirrun watched them now and then through hours of bumping and swaying. Mostly he looked from the air-cooled cocoon of the bus at the country shimmering in its heat haze. Ice on his water-bag. . . .

At sunset the bus rolled through a gateway in ranges of jumbled rock, and into Alice Springs. The Happy Folk collected their baggage and vanished into motels. Wirrun found an open shop and bought a few supplies. Then he walked out of the town, over dried-grass flats to the ghost gums beside the empty river. He knew where to look for the People.

There were a few of them just over the lip of the bank: two men with their wives and four or five tumbling children, and one much older man with proud dark eyes. The younger men had cans of beer and the old man a pipe. The women sat dark and shapeless, watching the children and waiting for the cool. Wirrun chose a gum that was not too far and not too near, and dropped his gear under it. He nodded to the men and threw oranges to the children, who scrambled for them, giggling. In a few minutes Wirrun went over to speak to their elders.

'All right if I camp here?' he asked.

'It's free here,' said the old man kindly, and the two younger men laughed.

'That's right, boy,' they said, turning it into a sneer. 'All free here.' Wirrun recognized the sneer and knew it was not meant for him.

They were not sure how to accept this grave, lean young stranger. So Wirrun talked about who he was and where he came from, and about his friend in the east who came from this country; and he told them where he had been and what he had seen; and their eyes grew warmer.

He asked about Mount Conner, and the old man said that that was his own country. Wirrun was delighted with this piece of good luck. He told about the swooping wind that died at night, and his camp last night, and the rich blue flower and the golden web, and the sunset behind the mountain; and the old man smiled and nodded. Then Wirrun told about the upside-down country and the ice.

The old man chuckled and puffed at his pipe. 'That's them Ninya,' he said. 'Terrible fellers, them Ninya.' And he looked sideways at Wirrun, but Wirrun only waited.

'They're all ice,' said the old man, puffing away. 'Ice beards, white frost all over. Ice in their caves. Under the ground, they are, and a big wind blowing in there.

Quiet nights, no wind outside, them Ninya comes out. Ice falls off'em. Cuts your feet in the morning. You can tell when you see them trees wrong side up. That means them Ninya's been out.' He looked sideways again. 'No men left to sing 'em back in their caves, put the trees back.'

Wirrun was silent, thinking of the frost-men in their caves of wind and ice. It was a satisfying story, big enough to explain that weird moment of morning; and yet it did not explain. Not quite. 'But it must be a bit late for 'em?' he suggested. 'Near summer. A bit hot for ice.'

The old men chuckled and chuckled, for it was a good joke on Wirrun. 'You camped in the wrong place,' he explained at last. 'That lake, that's right over their home. That rock's where they go in and out.'

All the People laughed, and Wirrun rolled his eyes and accepted the joke. When it was over he tried again, fingering the uneasiness inside himself. 'And now there's no one to keep 'em in order. Any chance they might get real bad?'

The old man puffed comfortably. 'They don't do no harm, you know,' he said. 'No one cutting their feet now, no one shivering. . . . Middle of summer, real hot, the women used to sing them out for a breeze. Good breeze then, nice and cool real quick. But they don't stay out long if it's hot.'

Wirrun nodded, and they talked about other things. The wind, which had died last night, was up tonight and singing in the ghost gums. They built a wind-break round their small fire, and the children curled up behind it and slept like puppies. Soon Wirrun said good night and went off to his own camp.

He wasn't really satisfied with the old man's account of the Ninya. Somewhere deep down, perhaps in his feet, he knew that a loved and beautiful country should not be left alone to battle against age and drought, heat and ice. It shouldn't be left to float upside down when the wind came. Maybe it wasn't. For it was very likely that the old man had told him only part of the tale.

'Not my business,' he reminded himself, lying in his sleeping-bag under the sharp bright stars. 'I told him any rate.'

The wind swooped over the ghost gums, and high over Wirrun it carried the Mimi tumbling in its waves.

All day the Mimi had eaten only seeds shaken from the grass and a few roots dug from under it. She had been sorrowful, thirsty, and distracted; it was too much to remember to be cautious too. So when a small lizard flickered from shade to shade she freed herself from the spinifex and pounced. Then she sat carelessly in a hollow of sand and ate the lizard. She was astonished when a gust of wind reached down and gathered her up.

She was tossed again from wind to wind, whirled high and circled lower. She had to learn all over again to ride the wind-waves with limbs and body safely held in line. She had her wits back by sunset, just as one broad deep shadow stole across the whole of the land.

For a moment she saw it: the land with no horizon, set forth in red and grey and slate. Empty rivers meandering into broad dry lakes of salt; hills ground down with age or baring jagged, hacked-out teeth; wind-built sandhills fold within fold; all stretching on and on till it melted in purple. The heart of the land as only the wind could see it, set forth with fearful honesty and a truth too plain to be believed. Then the shadow came, and even the Mimi's possum eyes could not see into it from so high.

It was good that she had to ride the wind with so much care; it kept her mind busy, and her terrors stood further back. Yet they stood all around. She saw in the darkness the brooding presence of spirits who belonged here where she had no right. She saw that she was carried always farther and farther from home, and her mind ran in terror from the question of how she might ever get back. And there was that worse terror that she didn't understand and dared not think of: the horror of the ice. The other fears had a tiny speck of hope in them: the spirits of this country might not mind so helpless a stranger blowing by under the stars; some day kind winds might come and carry her home. But she must not think of the ice.

Daylight came and she was wrapped in mist. Through wispy gaps she saw, very far down, the striding feet of dust-devils. All that day she was rolled in the soft white nothing of cloud and felt that she could neither breathe nor see. At night she came out of the cloud and was bewildered—she was between stars! There were white stars above and constellations of yellow below.

In the morning she was amazed again: she was passing over green country, and it was all divided into neat angular shapes. There was the shine of water in rivers, there were cloudy green heads of forests. But here and there were dead patches, like a lichen growing over the land; and even these were neatly cut into sections with straight black lines. Along the lines a kind of beetle swarmed and scuttled, shining and many-coloured. It was very strange country. The Mimi had little time to stare at it; the winds grew wayward and troublesome again and she was whirled back and forth, high and low, as at the beginning. She was giddy and weary and hopeless, and could only fight to hold on to her arms and legs.

In the late afternoon a broad band of hills rose gently, stretching away up and down the land. The wind rolled upward in a climbing wave, and she saw that these hills were not gentle; they were cleft deep into cliffs and had shadowed gorges and steep narrow valleys. Over these the wind tumbled and rolled, there was no pattern to it. The Mimi lost all sense of control—and found herself eddied backwards and tumbling down. She had fallen out of the wind.

Like a very long twig she came planing down a steep face of rock and scrub. A rise of warmer air lifted her—she stretched out her hands to a boulder, caught at a ledge, and hung weak and giddy. Now she was afraid of strange rocks and what they might contain—but the wind might loop down at her again, and she

knew only one thing to do. She breathed on the rock
and it opened its dark heart to her.

The Mimi fell into it and breathed it closed.

For two nights and a day she lay in the thick stillness
waiting for something terrible to happen. It did not.
The rock held her safely; it was black and still, neither
warm nor cold.

On the second day she moved her arms and legs
about, learning to use them again. On the third day she
ventured out. She found roots and water and caught a
bushrat, and ate and drank. Then she slipped back
quickly into the rock.

She was infinitely alone—banished she didn't know
where—and at night she wailed for the far, dear country of home. But this one rock held the safety of home.

And only a little way to the south, Wirrun too was at
home. He was sitting on the bed in his rented room
with a newspaper spread over his knees. The yellow
light of an electric bulb spilled over the print, and Wirrun read one small paragraph over and over. His dark
face was heavy with astonishment.

It was strange enough for astonishment. The air in
the room was warm and heavy, and this newspaper had
already recorded the warmest spring for twenty years.
Yet this small paragraph, tucked into the financial
pages to fill up a space, told of a sudden frost in
Queensland.

Three

For a young man of the People, a rented room in the Happy Folk's town was hardly home; but one of the things that Wirrun in his short life had never found was the place, the one spot in all the land, that was home. It may have been this that kept him thinking more than most young people of his years.

At any rate, he was back in the town he had left. He had travelled more comfortably than the Mimi, by plane, and had arrived a day or so earlier. He had pinned his used plane-ticket on the wall to celebrate, put away his camping gear, and settled down to save more money.

At the service station they had welcomed him back with all the proper jokes.

'Got used to living like a lord pretty quick, didn't he?'

'Collar-proud, eh? We'll soon knock that out of you.'

Wirrun had smiled his young white smile and hosed down floors and measured petrol and given change. And at night, because he was saving money for the next trip, he had gone home alone to cook his own dinner in his room, taking the newspaper to read. There he sat now, under the yellow bulb, staring at that small astonishing paragraph.

There was a small heading, PUZZLED INLANDER; and under it:

Mr George Jennings is a puzzled man. While the temperature soars and the summer promises to be the warmest for years, how did a small area of frost develop on his farm near Toowoomba on the Darling Downs? Mr Jennings claims to have discovered the phenomenon when bringing his cattle in for milking on Tuesday morning. After yarding the cattle he returned at once with a camera but found the frost had melted and was unfortunately unable to produce any evidence of his claim. 'It was in a little hollow between outcrops of rock,' Mr Jennings claimed. 'It's a bad spot for frost, but in fifty years I've never seen it this late.'

'Claims to have discovered . . . unable to produce any evidence.' It seemed to Wirrun that the newspaper did not believe the story. He was a student of newspapers. He thought that this one had had an empty space to fill, and had used an amusing story from a country newspaper. Perhaps that was the answer: the frost hadn't really happened. Yet Wirrun found it harder to believe that an Inlander would invent such a tale. A cabbage six feet round . . . a shark in the water-hole or an escaped lion in the scrub . . . a flying saucer landing in the swamp . . . it might tickle a dry Inlander's humour to fool the Happy Folk with tales like those. Frost in a warm October was a different matter, more serious.

He called up a picture of an Inlander face. It would have the settled look that came of never questioning anything it already knew. It was a cheerful face, but it could harden easily. It would harden a little at any mention of the Happy Folk, for the Inlander knew with hurt that the Happy Folk had abandoned him in favour of more impressionable peoples over the sea. But mostly the face was hardened by facing realities close at hand: realities of the land, the weather, and the bank. There was deep bitterness between the Inlanders and the People, but at least you knew their realities were real. On the question of frost on his own farm, this George Jennings had to be believed. Wirrun could only shrug and say what he had said once before.

'You'll get funny weather any time.'

He said it without thinking—but when he had said it the newspaper dropped to the floor. In his wanderings Wirrun had been north just as far as the Darling Downs. Toowoomba, on the edge of the escarpment . . . it could be cold in winter . . . in a freak summer too, maybe . . . but in the warmest spring for twenty years? *You'll get funny weather any time*; and the great quiet country floating upside down, and ice on his water-bag . . . He went to bed remembering his night under the ghost gums with the People. Already it was strange to remember.

There was no such quietness in town. The Happy Folk were in more than their usual frenzy, for Christmas was only weeks away and after Christmas there would be the summer sales. The streets were crowded, and there were big bright signs all over the town. GIVE HER A LITTLE HAPPINESS, they suggested, and offered it in a plastic bottle deliciously perfumed. BE HAPPY THE UNITED WAY—10% ON YOUR SAVINGS, they offered with a gleam in their eyes. YOU TOO CAN AFFORD FUR, they promised while the pavements were melting in the heat. And every night Wirrun, at home with his newspaper, followed the doings of the Folk when they were not buying or selling.

They were a study, these Folk. They dragged themselves, exhausted by heat, through ordeals of running and batting for the happiness of being top. They drowned themselves in pools for the happiness of owning pools. They cheated each other for the happiness of being rich, told lies for the happiness of being important, fought bitterly for the happiness of being right. Young Folk, taught in childhood, took what they fancied from other Folk, used it for an hour or so, and threw it away. One man killed another for the happiness of fifty dollars.

Wirrun read and wondered. He knew his own stern People would not have tolerated so primitive and destructive a happiness. He read his paper with care every night. That was how, within three or four days, he found another small heading: UNSEASONABLE WEATHER IN NEW ENGLAND.

He read the brief story, and his fingers and toes began to prickle. A patch of frost had been seen at Tenterfield. The paragraph was very like the one from Toowoomba; but at Tenterfield, as well as frost, a thin glazing of ice had formed on the drinking troughs of fowls. The newspaper made no mention of the earlier frost. Could only Wirrun have noticed that there were two? Two patches of frost late in a warm spring, and not very far apart. . . .

He put the paper down and went to riffle through his collection of maps. He thought the two places could hardly be more than a hundred miles apart. They were both in the high country, where in some years there might be a frost close to Christmas. Wirrun went back to the paper and checked the weather report. As far as he could tell, 'warm to hot and sunny' seemed to cover both areas.

He sorted through his maps with restless hands, laying them out and putting them together again. His fingers and toes still prickled. *Funny weather*; too funny. And too often. And too close.

'Not my business,' he said uneasily. It made him feel no better—for that too he had said before, in the great quiet centre of the land.

At last he stood up and shook himself impatiently. 'Too much shut up by myself. I should've seen Ularra before this. He'll want to hear about the trip.'

Ularra was the friend who had come from the red country, and whose talk of it had sent Wirrun there. Wirrun tracked him to a milk-bar and was greeted with a joyful shout. Ularra's skin was even darker than Wirrun's. He was tall and loose, not yet having learnt to manage his length. In the same way he talked loudly and laughed a lot, not yet having learnt to manage his feelings.

There was a table in the corner of the milk-bar. They sat there with glasses and straws and talked for a long time. Wirrun told about his trip, and Ularra's eyes shone. He laughed so loudly that Wirrun was sorry for his homesickness. But his voice dropped when he started to talk, drawing maps on the table, enlarging the trip and making it come to life again. Wirrun's eyes shone too.

'You know Mount Conner?' asked Wirrun, for the west is very wide. Ularra said of course he knew it, been there often, all down those salt lakes to Conner. Yet Wirrun knew that it was not really Ularra's country, and it turned out that he hadn't heard of the Ninya. So Wirrun told of his camp by the lake and his talk to the old man in Alice.

Ularra listened, nodded, but said nothing. It wasn't his business any more than it was Wirrun's.

'Funny thing, though,' said Wirrun; and he told about the newspaper reports of frost in Toowoomba and Tenterfield.

Ularra laughed loudly. 'Cheeky devils!' he said. 'No harm though. A bit of frost won't hurt.' With his eyes on Wirrun's face he shook his head. 'That's a long way, man, from Conner to Toowoomba. Never knew anyone make that trip, not straight across. What would it take walking? Couple of months?'

'Walking straight across you wouldn't make it,' said Wirrun, nodding. They talked about other things till the milk-bar had emptied and they had to go.

They stood on the pavement, Ularra's long arm thrown loosely over Wirrun's shoulder; the red country in the west had made them brothers, at least for tonight. Wirrun's uneasiness had almost gone; but when he felt a flick of its tail he spoke at once. He didn't care if Ularra grinned.

'You know some of them out there,' he said. 'Got a name and address for any of the Mount Conner men?'

Ularra didn't grin. 'I might,' he said. 'There's a bloke in Alice'd know any rate. Want me to see?'

'You do,' said Wirrun. 'I might need to write.' He went home feeling that he had done what was needed, and slept soundly.

And the next evening he found another small strange

paragraph in the newspaper: FREAK FROST AT EMMA-
VILLE.

Wirrun knew about Emmaville and its tin mines:
south of Tenterfield, on the western side of the plateau.
The two places were so close that the paper had treated
both frosts as one, but Wirrun noticed there had been a
day between them. Only one day and a few miles between two frosts? What were they up to now?

What were who up to? He was suddenly angry, either
with himself or with the frosts. Ularra was right: a little
frost, a bit of thin ice, what harm could it do in warm
weather? The women of Mount Conner would have
called it up for a breeze.

But the women were not there now to call up the
Ninya. And the men were not there to sing them back.
And no one else would know the right songs.

And still, what harm could they do?

Wirrun never threw away his old papers too soon. He
found the earlier reports of frost, cut out all three,
pasted them together on a sheet from his writing-pad,
and put that away with his maps. He did all this angrily,
as though someone else had nagged him into doing it;
and he found a point that he seized on with an angry
'Ha!'

None of the stories said anything about the country
floating upside down in the air. Not one word about any
mirage. That was it, then. The Ninya were safe at home
and they were having funny weather up north. He went
to bed in triumph.

But just as he was falling asleep a voice, maybe his
own, spoke in his mind: 'They shoulda got up earlier
and they'd have seen it floating.'

The next day's paper gave him no trouble. It was full
of the Happy Folk's frenzy, and advice about Christmas
spending. At the service station, in the boss's little office, a large plastic Santa Claus and a tinsel tree were
propped behind the door, ready to be used for decora-
tions at the first permissible moment. Wirrun turned his
mind to Christmas, and friends to whom he might send
a card or a gift. It was four days before the paper both-

ered him again, and this time the paragraph was easily
seen. It was nearer the front of the paper and had a
bigger heading than the others: SUMMER FREEZE ON
TABLELANDS.

The hair on the nape of Wirrun's neck crawled a little as he read.

Mystery surrounds the reported appearance during
the week of freak frosts at Toowoomba on the Darling Downs in Queensland and at Emmaville and
Tenterfield on the Northern Tablelands of New
South Wales. Yesterday a fresh report came from
Glen Innes, also on the Tablelands. This year's un-
usually high temperatures have prevailed throughout
the area and the Weather Bureau is unable to offer
an explanation. 'These are unconfirmed reports,' said
one of its officers. 'We have to consider the extreme
unlikelihood of frost in prevailing conditions. You
could say that these reports have much in common
with reports of flying saucers.' But from his farm
near Glen Innes Mr Warren Jones claims. . . .

Wirrun read on. Frost on a rocky hillside, thin ice on
a dam. He cut out this story to add to the others on his
sheet of paper and stayed for a moment staring at his
maps.

It was coming south, then; coming down a route
along the high rocky country of the Tablelands. What
deep caverns might run through those rocks, and for how
many miles? If you were the Ninya you could find
them.

He took out some of the maps, and an atlas he had
kept from school. He thought there was high rock-
based country running all the way from Mount Conner,
first north and then east into Queensland, and curving
round to the Downs near the coast. But no one had
talked about frost along all those thousands of miles;
and no mirage, no floating country. The Weather Bureau was right. It was just the same as flying saucers,
and he was as bad as anyone.

But staring at the map he knew he was making excuses, shutting his eyes and refusing to see, like the Happy Folk. Not many people had seen those miles, but everyone knew about them. The Simpson desert, the channel country . . . at night it would be all black, with maybe one dot of light here and maybe another a hundred miles away. No wonder if nobody happened to see a small patch of frost, gone in an hour. And suppose anyone did? He would talk about it by radio to his Inlander neighbours. He wouldn't write to the papers—and if he did they wouldn't print it. It was too far away from the cities of the Happy Folk; they couldn't possibly understand that it mattered. Only an Inlander, any Inlander, would know that.

He put his maps back with the newspaper story and smiled grimly at the thought of four tight-lipped Inlanders reading it. 'Flying saucers,' they would mutter in disgust. 'Typical, isn't it?' Wirrun suddenly thought that if he wanted a white man's help in a matter like this the man had better be an Inlander.

Only he didn't want help. He still didn't see what harm a little frost could do, and it wasn't his business. The most he could do was to send some word to Mount Conner; and what word could he send?

He lay in bed and wondered how many frosts there had been, and where; how far apart, how many days between. How far south would they come, and when? Where were they heading?

He woke up saying, 'But I don't know the songs.'

It didn't make any difference. He knew he would have to go. Maybe he didn't know what harm there was in a little frost—but he knew there was harm. Maybe he didn't know the songs, but he was the one easterner who knew about the Ninya. Maybe he was wasting his time, but how did he know till he started? He had breakfast and set to work.

He took his saved-up money from the place behind the dresser. Only forty dollars yet: it would have to do. He cleaned out the shabby refrigerator and switched off its noisy motor, packed a few supplies with his oldest shirts and shorts, and rolled up his gear ready for travel. Then he locked his room, put the key over the door, and went to the service station to speak to the boss.

He knew this would be bad. The Happy Folk might grumble about their work as much as they chose, but they knew it made their little world stick together. You held a job and pulled your weight or you poled on other people. Jobs were for sticking to, and Wirrun was full of guilt as he spoke to the boss.

The boss was amazed and stern. 'Not good enough. You're only just back, and there's young David off next week. You can't keep a job and go walkabout whenever you feel like it.'

'That's right,' muttered Wirrun. 'It's bad, that. Only I gotta go. Business.' He hoped for much from that magic word, but the boss only snorted.

'Too much money, that's what it is. I've got a business to run, too. You can get into your overalls and get yourself started or you needn't come back at all.'

'Sorry, boss,' said Wirrun; and he was sorry, and acutely embarrassed as well. 'It's a good job here. But I gotta go.'

He took the small final pay that the boss snatched out of the cash register and walked away from his job. It was worrying, but when he got back would be the time to worry. Now he had to find Ularra.

Ularra worked in a factory and would not be out till midday lunch. Wirrun bought more supplies while he waited. He was there when Ularra came slouching out of the factory, straightening up with a grin when he saw Wirrun.

Wirrun explained as quickly and as much as he could. Ularra listened thoughtfully and nodded. 'But what's the harm?' he asked, a little puzzled.

'I don't *know* what harm. Somebody's got to keep an eye, haven't they? You can see that. Did you find that address?"

Ularra had found the address of the bloke in Alice and thought he could get word quick to the men of

Mount Conner if Wirrun found the word to send. He promised to wait for a message from Wirrun, and to send it on fast if the men were wanted. They said good-bye solemnly.

Wirrun set off for the railway station. His only plan was to take a train as far up the Tablelands as his money would allow, and then to start walking. He would watch the newspapers for news of the frosts, and sooner or later he thought he would see one for himself. He would try to discover and follow the route of the frosts. What then, he didn't know. But when he reached the station the afternoon papers were out and he bought one at once. The story was on page two, with a bigger headline than before.

FREAK FREEZE COMES SOUTH?

The story altered his plans while he read it. It came from the high country near Dorrigo . . . Dorrigo! That was east as well as south! And so much nearer! It would have been a mistake to go up the Tablelands, or to go too far in any direction; he could have overshot his mark. . . . Some ice and a heavy frost, 'more like snow', the farmer had said. And he had added a phrase that Wirrun read sharp-eyed: "There was a funny sort of shine to it.'

A funny sort of shine: like the cellophane shimmer of the country when it floated upside down?

He dropped the paper into a bin and stood thinking for a moment. The frost had turned to the coast, maybe towards his own country. He thought of places where high and rocky hills came near the sea. Port Macquarie might be too far up . . . somewhere near the Hunter, maybe . . . a quiet place in the bush where he could strike north or west or south . . . with a post office handy, for his message to Ularra. He went to buy his ticket.

Soon the train, swaying and beating its song-sticks in the unchanging rhythm of trains, was carrying him on the short journey north. In a little while he would leave it and walk inland, a young man of the People in search of a mountain.

Four

And much farther north a mountain groaned. It was full of a heaviness and chill it had long forgotten. Deep inside it a cold wind howled, freezing the bones of the mountain as it went. There was a stream, never seen or heard, though its sound had silvered the dark for an age of time; it grew silent now, and fretted into ice. There was a lake, cool and liquid in the dark for a thousand years; now it had hardened into ice in a frosty twilight. The wind howled on ahead, and the Ninya walked in the mountain.

They glittered with the purity of frost; crystals like diamonds dropped from their beards; and they snarled at each other for company.

'A wasted search, led by the earless.'

'Truly I am a fool, to lead those who fret like the children of the People. Lead yourselves, then—into the fire.'

'And where is that? We travel as blind as ants in a crack. Who knows where the Eldest Nargun lives?'

'I know, and I lead you there. The Eldest lives by the sea, and south, in its country.'

There was snapping laughter and a chorus of creaks.

'By the sea. And south. And in its country. Now we know all.'

'The sea is long, oh Leader of the Ninya. The south is wide. The countries are forgotten.'

'To walk on and on is not to search. I see a rock: is that the Nargun? I see a cave: is the Eldest in there? Tell us, Clever One.'

'Look for yourselves—what holds you back? I, who lead you, I think and need not look.'

'Tell us what you think then, Great One.'

'Must I tell you again, like children? If the Eldest were here, would it not have seen the first blooming of frost? And would it hide in a cave and freeze? I tell you it would stand here now, in our path, and these cold rocks would glow red.'

They muttered sullenly.

'Listen again, you who cannot think. If the Nargun were in any country we have passed, if it were anywhere within knowing, it would stand here now and your white blood would trickle in the stream. So do not look in caves like hunters of bats but look at the ice. Feel the air, and the flowing of the wind. If one drop of water gathers on a spear of ice—if the wind only falters for a moment—it is time for work.'

There were creaking whispers and sharp glances all around. The leader nodded.

'Come, then. South by the coast. We hunt no bat in a cave but the Nargun. To ring it with frost and work a sudden wonder of ice. To call down snow and crack the old bones of the Eldest. To see the land white again in the sun, and the glory of sun on a glacier. No changeless frost in a twilit cave but the delicate melting and building again, with the air breathing white.'

All the Ninya broke into chanting, and the wind howled with them, and the leader felt it with care. And far to the south, off the shore of its own country, the Eldest Nargun felt the sea.

The sea flowed over and round it, tugging. The Nargun spread itself a little and gripped at rock. All its senses were sharply alert, fixed on another movement. Somewhere in the water there was a quickness of life, and the Nargun was hungry.

Only five years had passed since its last meal; once it would have been twenty or fifty. But the old thing hungered oftener now, and the sea could not satisfy it. Life in the sea was slyer, colder, quicker, than life on the land; or it was sly and cold and slow. Nothing moved the ancient monster to love any more; only to yearning. So it hungered often, and seized what the sea brought near.

Something flicked and nibbled at the weeds on its side. The Nargun crouched and waited, with the slow enduring patience of stone. The fish nibbled again—flicked away from a streak of foam—nuzzled back. The Nargun crouched, balancing its weight against the pull of the tide as the sea had taught it.

A wave pushed in and pulled out, and the weed swayed with it. The Nargun moved too: a secret movement, lighter than a leaf. Now it was poised. The fish hovered and stayed.

A ripple flashed in the sun: with that same speed and light the Nargun moved. There was shock and stillness in the water, and a mist of blood and white flesh. Nothing else was left. Nothing flicked and nibbled at the Nargun's side.

With the next wave the old monster rocked back and cried, 'Nga-a!' It spread its weight again and gripped the rock and rested. A glint of green-gold light wavered over it, and a faint warmth from the sun.

The ancient stone lay still and dreamed of fire.

2

On the Mountain

One

Wirrun found a dusty road and walked inland, hoping he had chosen well. Was he too far up the coast or too far down? Was he right in choosing the coast at all, or in choosing a lonely height behind the coast? Maybe the frost would leave the heights and be seen in one of the towns. Maybe it could travel in a flash and appear tomorrow a hundred miles to the south. Maybe it would pause and stay where it was for a month or a year. He could find no answers to these questions, but as he walked he remembered that there were no answers. He remembered what he was: a young man alone, looking for a mountain.

He found a company of them, standing above a village on a ridge. Their volcanic tops were roughly draped in scrub and their lower slopes hung with forest. For a moment he wavered, uncertain which to choose; but he could have sat and thought for an hour, inventing some reason for a choice. Instead he started to climb.

The slope steepened rapidly. He was stepping on boulders buried in grass and creeper, winding his way up between grey box and stringybark. The upper heights, when he reached them, seemed all rock; but the scrub had found pockets of leaf-mould and clay. He came upon an overhanging ledge of rock. From its nearest end he could look down at the village. He went along its length, further round the side of the mountain, and stowed his gear under the ledge and built his fireplace. It would be hidden from the village.

The sun was low already. He had only time to explore a little around his camp, but he had to find water. He looked for a gully, and found one that at any other time he would have thought too far—he would have had to move his camp nearer. But he liked the camp he had found, and he expected to be walking every day around this mountain; he could always fill a water-bag on the way.

The gully was steep and rockbound with a trickle of water slipping through stones in its bed. A little scrub timber grew there, tallow-wood and sycamore, with tree-ferns and small ferns and moss. It was steep and narrow, shutting out the sun; but it was easy enough to climb into if you went to the right place. He took some water back to his camp and lit his fire.

He slept soundly that night, tired after walking, till the early sun struck under the ledge at his face. It was too late by then to look for frost. He spent his first day walking over and round the mountain, finding out about it and working out a route. Always, like a man of the People, he moved under cover of shadow and rock and scrub. If the Inlanders saw him they would narrow their eyes and watch; then they would judge in terms of their own hard realities.

At first he thought like a bushman, noting the chain of ridges that tied the peaks together, examining faces of slippery rock and slopes of falling stone. He found his way into deep and shady places all around the mountain, climbed over ledges and into the heads of gullies. After a time it seemed that he had stopped thinking at all; or perhaps he was thinking with his feet.

In the afternoon he went down to the village, circling from tree to tree and coming in from the opposite direction. He bought a paper and sat under a tree to read it. There were no more reports of frost, but the Happy Folk were having fun at the expense of the Inlanders. ATTACK FROM OUTER SPACE? . . . SANTA ESTABLISH-ING POLAR OUTPOSTS . . . and so on. The merrymakers were supported by the opinion of a learned man. Wirrun left the paper behind in a bin and returned by his roundabout route to the mountain.

On the second day he began a round of the mountain in the colourless shadowless dawn. It was cold, but not too cold for an early November morning. He went into all the hidden places, feeling and seeing. He found no frost, but as the sun rose he found the mountain: rock and cone-tree, moss in its damp places, the violet poised, the clematis twining and coiling.

I am Land, the First Thing. Serve me, said the mountain.

'That's what I came for,' said Wirrun. He saw gold of wattle and silver under grevillia leaves, shadow and wind and the heat-stroke of sun on rock. He heard spiders scuttle and owls sleep, felt the lizard twitch under the bark and the snake slither under the stone.

He walked the mountain till late afternoon and lay among ferns to rest. He saw the reflected sunset turn the eastern haze to fire; and at night he sat close to his own small fire and listened to the mountain.

Frost grows by night and melts by day, said the mountain.

'Tomorrow,' said Wirrun, 'I'll sleep first and go about in the night.'

Peering around the ledge, the Mimi heard him. She had seen him much earlier and remembered him sleeping by the saltpan in the west. It made her all the more anxious and she tracked him through the day with great caution, always sliding near rock. She thought Wirrun had the look of a man who might soon see earth-spirits, even a Mimi.

The peace that the Mimi had found in her rock had not lasted long. She had slipped out of it and travelled along the ridges trying rock after rock. She could not be at peace for long in any of them. She was forced to spend most of her time on the outside, nervously sheltering from sudden breaths of wind, ready at a rustle to slip inside; and then as soon as she could she must slip out again.

For when the safe black silence of rock folded close, the Mimi thought there were noises in it: noises too faint and far for even her quivering ears to catch. The

deep-down plinking of a hidden stream she knew; and
the footstep of a spider; and the falling of dust. She
could be at ease with those. But when they were still—
what was that tremble of rock, as though somewhere in
the mountains something creaked? What was that rustle, dry and cold and faint, *rrsh*, like a mouse-claw in
sand? And why did the air stir and whisper a word?
Caverns should not breathe. The Mimi lay stiff, straining her ears past their limit. If she did sleep she
dreamed of wind, and the rustle of frost, and the creak
of ice.

She began to look for some home outside the rock, a
hollow log or a hole in a tree. She saw Wirrun and followed him till he slept, then went on with her search. It
was hard both to search and to gather food when she
dared not go two paces from rock for fear of the wind.

In the morning Wirrun made his early round of the
mountain and found only the dawn cold and no sense
of ambush. In the afternoon he made his silent visit to
the village, then ate and slept. He slept into the night,
till the white stars of the Cross had swung far over and
the yellow lights of the village had blinked out. He fed
his fire and banked it deep in ashes, then started his
night round.

The night is not quiet. It pulsed with the singing of
crickets, and some tiny insect rang a bell as clear as a
bell-bird's, over and over. Lower down the mountain a
koala cried. Possums swore and squabbled, or breathed
heavily to themselves like asthmatic old men. A wallaby
thumped, a bushrat scuttled, a moth beat the air. All
the soft scurry of the night was woven into a fabric of
sound that hung across the mountain like a curtain; but
Wirrun listened to the mountain.

The ice is coming, said the mountain.

'I can't find it,' said Wirrun. He slid from bush to
thicket, resting his hands on rock and feeling shadows.
He could still find no sense of ambush or any black
cold, but he felt the awareness of the night. It was
breathing and waiting.

There was something watching in the night: something larger and quieter than cricket or wallaby. Did the darkness thin and thicken, swirling in clouds? What followed him?

Look ahead, said the mountain, *for the ice is coming*.

And Wirrun went on, fixing his mind on the route that he had to find again by night; but it wasn't the ice he felt. Some tingling in his hands and feet, and at the centre of his forehead, told him that he was followed.

He skirted rock-faces and slopes of stone, feeling his way. He found the entrance to the gully and climbed in and out. And the darkness thickened behind him and thinned when he looked back. At last he drew near his camp-fire again, and stopped to lay more wood on the coals and draw them together. It was warm and safe by the fire; he longed to stay there, but the mountain called. He must go round again.

He started, and the darkness thickened ahead, and he forced himself to walk into it. Step by step, step by step, while his hands and feet and the centre of his forehead tingled. He felt a chill and thought it must be the ice, but it was a sound that did not belong to the scurry of night noises: a clear trilling that came from where the dark was thickest. Wirrun turned that way and stood still. The dark came to him.

It looked like a man of the People, but its eyes were red and it grinned. It carried a great pointed nulla-nulla, too heavy for a man. It held out the nulla-nulla to Wirrun.

'We fight,' it said. 'You strike first.' And it bent its head for a blow.

He knew he must not touch the nulla-nulla. He knew he must run, but he stood shocked and shaking. The shape of dark seemed to gather and thicken over him.

He tore himself free of it and turned and ran for the camp-fire. He could feel the dark shape running and grinning behind, and hear it trilling. He turned his head desperately and shouted: 'The ice is coming!' The thing faltered, and Wirrun bounded to the fire.

He dropped down by it and reached for wood to pile on and make a blaze. He had to keep looking into the dark but nothing came out of it. Then the flames leapt up, and the dark stepped back and stood around the fire a little way off. When the flames sank down it breathed forward, and when they rose it shrank back. Wirrun fed the fire till the dark grew watery because morning was near. Then he banked the fire down and crept into his sleeping-bag. He could see all the shapes near by, and they were trees.

'Bones gone squashy,' he told himself weakly. 'That's a nice thing. You come looking for—things—and when you meet 'em you run like a rabbit.' But he hadn't thought of meeting them. He wondered what had happened to men of the People who had met this shape of dark, who had taken the offered club and given the blow. He shuddered.

These too I have bred, said the mountain.

'Old sinner,' muttered Wirrun. He didn't like what the mountain said but it had to be thought about. He lay while the sun rose and the land grew warm, wondering how many dark earth-creatures the mountain had bred in all the ages of its cooling and weathering. By the time he crawled out to cook some breakfast he knew that however many there were, and however terrible, they had to be accepted. You couldn't choose to have the rocks and ferns and moss and the green shadows but reject the cliffs and the snake. He didn't like it, but the ice was coming. He would walk the mountain again at night if he could, and run if he had to run.

'Any rate,' he remembered, 'that old one didn't like the ice either.' And he wondered what it was that the old thing disliked. That the Ninya were coming out of the west into its own country? Or the ice itself?

He went early to the village for his paper and found he was too early. He had to wait till a truck had brought the papers in from an early train. Sitting under a tree and waiting he thought that he didn't really need the paper now. The ice was coming: the mountain, or the land itself, had told him that through his fingers and feet and the centre of his forehead. It was settled and known. The Ninya were bringing the ice, bringing it

here, and it was not a little thing that melted in an hour.
It was a power of ice advancing. He wondered if he
should tell Ularra to send for the Mount Conner men at
once; but he still didn't know when the ice would come,
or where or how long it might halt on the way.

A cloud of dust came along the road with a truck
mixed up in it. Wirrun watched it roll up to the shop
and waited while bundles and cases from the train were
carted inside. Then he went and bought his paper.

More frost had been found, yesterday morning,
about sixty miles nearer and still close to the coast. This
time the Inlander who found it had left his stock and
called out his wife and a neighbour. The neighbour had
brought a camera, so the combined witnesses could not
easily be dismissed. The Happy Folk were irritated by
this, and would soon be looking for someone to blame.
Wirrun smiled a little as he cut out the article and
dropped the paper into a bin. The Happy Folk seemed
to have grown smaller since he left them; from the
mountain they looked like children.

The night and the morning had tired him. He went
back to the mountain and slept through the rest of the
day. The Mimi peeped at him from her tree before she
ventured out for food. He was sound asleep.

He woke to stars and the billowing dark and the fabric of noises curtaining the night. He looked down at
the village lights and up at the shapes of mountains
against the stars, and he felt the land reach for him and
take him. His fear of the night tingled like an old nettle-
sting; but he ate, banked his fire, and set out to walk
the mountain.

It was a long walking, while the darkness gathered
and thinned and Wirrun's skin crawled. He listened and
felt, and crawled into all the deepest places to test the
shadows, and found no sudden bite of cold.

The wind comes, said the mountain.

Wirrun stood still and listened, but the night was
calm without any stirring of leaves. There was no wind;
yet he felt in his feet the faraway howling of a gale. He
went on troubled.

He was on the steeper face of the mountain and far from his fire when the dark gathered and pursued him. It came at him in the shape of a woman with a long horn pointing up from each shoulder. It shook its shoulders, grinned wickedly, and bent over to run at him with lowered horns.

Wirrun ran, but he knew with terror that he could not run far on this slope without falling. He dived through a thicket, hoping that the long horns would tangle in branches, but the woman-shape flowed through it like water, grinning after him.

'The ice is coming!' shrieked Wirrun. 'Why don't you run at that?'

The shape faltered and shook its horns, and he slid away trembling to hide in a cleft of rock. But he went on, and made two rounds of the mountain, finding nothing.

He went wearily back to his fire in the pearl-shell dawn and ate and slept. He woke in the evening, tight with tension, wishing for the first time that he could go away and leave the mountain to itself. Yet when he tried to think of going it seemed there was nowhere to go and nothing to do. All the land was closed to him except this one perch on the mountain.

He made himself a meal and sat over it listlessly, not wanting to move and yet itching and twitching with nerves. For hours after the meal was finished he sat by the fire twisting a straw of grass round and round one finger. The night wore on and the mountain called, but like a sulky child he refused to hear.

The mountain groaned.

Wirrun gave in with a bad grace, dragged his fire together, and went like a sulky child, muttering.

'Shoulda brought a firestick if I had the sense of a rabbit. What's the good of a man that can't even carry a firestick? Cold—cripes!'

The Mimi watched him in terror. She had ventured into the rock an hour ago and had tumbled out quivering. She had been quivering ever since.

As Wirrun walked his mind awoke from sulkiness

but the brooding anxiety grew worse. For one thing, as he grew more alert he discovered the silence. No fabric of small noises hung over the mountain tonight. The silence was deep and shocking. It frightened him. For another thing, he found that he was not in fact cold yet still he longed for a firestick. He wondered what terror worse than the horned woman waited for him in this night.

I freeze, said the mountain.

Wirrun searched and searched, but he could not find the cold.

He went into all the deep and shadowed places, and the clefts of damp rock, feeling and testing. He lingered in the gully where the water trickled; his hands and feet and the centre of his forehead tingled, but he could find nothing. He climbed out again, muttering.

He stood like a shadow in a patch of scrub and listened to the silence. He wanted badly to go back to his fire. When the silence cracked into sound he shuddered and shrank back. The sound came closer, *crack . . . crack,* a measured beat like the thump of a wallaby but loud and sharp; and with it came a strange cry, *'Pirralog! Pirralog!'*

He knew it was an earth-creature and shivered. This must be it, the worst thing, the thing he had felt and dreaded. Yet he couldn't run. He saw it gather out of the darkness, bounding like a kangaroo, but in shape and size more like a horse. It had a sort of mane on its neck and its tail was like a long sharp knife. It saw him: its neck reached for him, its fierce eyes cut the dark, and it bounded again. And still his fear weighted Wirrun's feet.

Then—the earth-thing stopped. It shifted restlessly; its head turned from side to side; it pawed at the ground. It had lost interest in Wirrun. It gave its cry once or twice, *'Pirralog! Pirralog!'* Then it turned and bounded off, and the sharp cracking faded.

That was indeed the worst. Wirrun knew it would have been better if the old thing had chased him. But the night lay heavy on it, as it did on Wirrun, and tonight it would not chase a man. He went on his way, pricking and tingling.

He came near his camp-fire again, and stopped to feed it and draw the coals together. The stars were wheeling towards morning. And suddenly Wirrun could not leave the fire—not yet— He crouched beside it watching the red pulse of the coals, and the fresh wood smoulder and catch. He felt the mountain groan and said sullenly, 'Not yet.'

He left the fire when the stars had thinned and trees and rocks were coming out of the dark. He went straight to the gully. It faced east, and the light was stronger there.

The ice lay in it. Its dark rocks glistened silver-grey with frost, and the ferns were silver-green. The trickling water lay in little pools of ice and in ridges of ice between the stones. Wirrun climbed carefully down to the slippery bed and scraped at the frost with his foot. The sun rose, and struck straight up the gully.

And it rose and floated above him, shimmering. Tree and rock and fern reached downward, groping for their proper place. Wirrun shut his eyes for a moment and then began to climb out, for he didn't know the right songs to put it back in place.

Two

Wirrun went back to his fire, and his mind was clouded with weariness and defeat. The Ninya had come and gone, and he knew no more than before. He had seen the ice, the great and terrible ice, and it was a little thing. And still it was terrible, and still he did not know why. He was only Wirrun, alone and not much more than a boy; he had done all that he could and it was useless.

'Not all,' he said bitterly as he crawled into his sleeping-bag. 'I shoulda gone sooner.'

He fell asleep like a worn-out child. He woke in terror, hurling through space with the wind screeching in his ears. He tried to shout but his throat had closed up as if he were choking. Something gripped him: a dark body painted with white markings. When he struggled it held him strongly as though he were a child and carried him on into the wind. There was nothing in the world but the wind and the dark, painted body—until Wirrun looked down, and tried again to give a choked cry. They were flying at eagle height above the trees.

Wirrun stopped struggling and tried instead to cling to the arms that held him. He was helpless in this dizzy rushing of air.

'Don't be afraid,' said a deep voice just over his head. 'I am Ko-in.'

When he managed to look up he could see a strong, stern face, a face of the People. He knew that one of the earth-creatures had caught him at last, and he lay weakly waiting for whatever might happen.

A great thickness of trees was coming at him from below. He was falling like a stone, he and the creature together. . . . Treetops grabbed at them, but they slipped between. The ground rushed at them, and while Wirrun waited for the crash they came safely and gently to earth. There was a fire deep under trees and Wirrun was laid beside it, choking and gasping.

He tried again to speak, and again he could not. His throat was closed, though he could breathe well enough. The earth-creature stood beside him, tall and dark, its body painted in a pattern of white pipeclay. It moved away—he should run, but he was too weak to stand. The creature came back, crouched beside him like a man, and laid some leaf on his lips.

'I am Ko-in,' it said again in its deep, grave voice. 'This is my fire. Speak with me.'

Wirrun found that he could speak now, but there

were not yet any words to say. Slowly he sat up. He
began to believe that this creature meant him no harm.
It had none of the fierce and dreadful look of the night-
things, and its eyes were like those of the oldest of the
People. He found that he wanted to speak, but all that
came was his one urgent message.

'The ice is coming.'

'The ice has come,' said Ko-in. 'It has taken its path
further on. Why do you hunt the ice?'

Wirrun tried to remember why. 'The land told me,'
he said.

'Ah,' said Ko-in as if all were explained. But all was
not explained, and Wirrun struggled to tell more.

'You think it's just a bit of frost. It looks small. But
it's big and terrible.'

'It has been a big and terrible ice in its time,' said
Ko-in. But he spoke as if for conversation's sake.

'It comes from another country in the west. The
Ninya brought it. And the People have gone, the ones
that should have sung the Ninya back.'

'There must be the People,' Ko-in agreed politely. It
angered Wirrun. He hadn't walked the mountain at
night and done all that he could to have his urgent message received politely.

'Now it's gone further on, out of your country,' he
said bitterly, 'so you don't care. Well, there's others of a
night, I've seen 'em. They don't look as good as you,
and maybe they can't fly, but any rate they care.'

Ko-in's grave brown eyes lit with a spark. 'You've
seen them,' he agreed, 'and they care. Ko-yo-rowen,
and Yaho with her horns, and Puttikan who bounds;
the old ones of the night. They dislike the ice; and they
dislike the Ninya who leave their own country and
come into ours. They are earth-things. But I am hero.
My care is a different kind. I care for the land when the
ice grips it and when the fire scorches it. How do you
care?'

Wirrun had never known, but in his fury he discovered now. He looked around him for words. The hills
—the sky—the sea—anyone could care for those.

He said, 'There's a dung-beetle by that log. I care for that. And there's a rotten toadstool with a worm in it: I care for both of 'em. I care for that bit of fern, and the little white men by the sea, and the horse-thing in the night. I care for the ice and the fire.'

Ko-in bent his head. 'You are of the People,' he said. 'We have talked very much, very long; we have talked so long that we have said everything. You have said everything, for you have said that the land told you. And I too have said everything, for I have said that there·must be the People. Now the talking is over and the doing begins. Put away your anger, for in this country and at this time you must not be angry with Ko-in.'

Wirrun stared at the ground. He was now too embarrassed for anger. He felt as people feel whenever they speak in anger: that he had said too little and too much and had failed to speak at all.

'I give you help in your hunting,' said Ko-in. 'Go to the place where the ice came. There is a cave in that gully, a small cave, a large hole in the rock. A man who was dying left in it a power of the People. Find it and keep it with you. Now sleep.'

At once Wirrun slept.

He woke by his own fire in the shade of the mountain, and knew by the shade that it was past noon. He felt rested and strong, not despairing, not even in need of a meal. He started at once for the village to send out his call for the men of Mount Conner.

As he went he thought with wonder of Ko-in, who was hero. Soon he would think about Ko-in's help and try to find it; but first he must do what was right. For this was a business of the People, and Ko-in himself had said that there must be the People. His own were not the right People for the Ninya, and their power was not the right power. Even if Wirrun found it after its long years of mouldering in a cave; even if he knew it when he found it; even if he dared to touch it! For among his People Wirrun had never been made a proper man.

He did not buy a paper in the village, for he knew

where the last frost had been. He sent his telegram to
Ularra: 'MEN WANTED SEND QUICK.' That was enough.
The post office would say where the message came
from, and Ularra would watch the papers for later
news. He hoped very much that the men would come
quickly. He thought they would come, for it was their
business; but it was a long way to come and it might be
hard for them. They might not have learnt the trick of
saving money and buying speed. Wirrun bought a few
things in the village and went back to the mountain.

Tonight there was no need to walk the mountain.
First, while it was still light, he would look for Ko-in's
help. Then he would think again about his own plans
and what he should do now that the ice had gone past.

He stowed his goods under the ledge and went on to
the gully, pausing on the lip to remember it as he had
seen it last. Now it lay cool and shadowed; evening had
come into it already. The water slid and whispered
through its stones but the ferns were black with frost.
Wirrun climbed into it, holding by a creeper here and
brushing past a tree-fern there, by the route he had
learnt to follow even at night. He went straight to the
steep wall of rock at its head for that was where the
small cave, the large hole, would be. But how would he
know the power?

He climbed as high as a man might who was dying
and needed to hide a power. Then he worked his way
across the rock, reaching into hollows and exploring
with his fingers. He might be looking for wood, carved
or painted or fingered smooth—and rotted away long
ago in its damp cave. He might be looking for stone,
and how would he know this one stone from all the
rest? He shut his eyes and let his mind flow into his
groping fingers. . . .

When he touched the power he knew it at once. It
was round, both soft and hard, and enclosed in coarse
net. He drew it out.

It was dark with age and damp, and with dust that
the damp had darkened. The outer bag was netted from
a strong twine of bark fibre. The round ball inside, both

soft and hard, was the size of a cricket ball: a closely wound ball of soft cord made from what he guessed was possum fur. Wirrun slung the net bag from his belt. As he did so he realized that that was what the bag was meant for; but the belt too would most likely have been of soft cord.

He climbed down from the rocks and out of the gully. The evening was spreading. He walked back to his camp with one hand closed over the power on his belt. It felt powerful; and old; but he didn't know what he should do with it. He didn't even know if he should take it out of its bag or unwind the soft cord. He left it hanging on his belt, for that much at least he knew was meant, and sat by his fire to eat and think.

He had done all that he knew: seen the ice and felt its power; sent for the men; found Ko-in's help. Tomorrow, he thought, he would have to leave this mountain and try to track the ice on its way south. That was all he could think of. At least he could mark its way for the men of Mount Conner. But he wished he knew where it was headed, and what its terror was. As for the People's power that hung at his belt, he didn't think it would really help very much. It was a power of this country which he must now leave. And Wirrun didn't even know what sort of power it was.

He put more wood on the fire and dragged the coals together. Then he took the power from his belt and left the net bag hanging in place. He sat by the fire with the power folded in his hands: he could feel in its roundness the swing of the hills, the cup of the valley, the arch of the sky, and the circling of the sea. He felt tall, tall as a tree.

The wood caught into red and yellow flame, and the dark stepped back. Wirrun looked out at it across his firelit space; and there at the edge of the breathing dark stood Ko-in with a firestick in his hand. The firelight caught him and lost him again as the dark breathed out and in.

'Come and talk,' said Ko-in, 'Clever One.'

'That's not me,' said Wirrun a little sternly. 'I'm not even a proper man.' But he got up from the fire to go, with the power in his hands. Ko-in watched him with the People's eyes, grave and gentle.

'And where are the proper men?' he asked. 'I have looked for them a long time. Are they here hunting the ice? I see only a boy who hears what the land tells; and who else is there now to speak and tell? I put the power of the People into the boy's hands.'

Wirrun halted in shock. 'But I can't,' he said.

'The power is in your hands and the land has told you. Will you refuse the land?'

'I've tried that,' said Wirrun. 'It didn't work.'

The firelight wavered, the dark breathed in and out, and Ko-in said again, 'Come and talk, Clever One.' Wirrun saw that behind him the dark gathered into other shapes. He saw the maned beast that bounded, and the woman with horned shoulders, and the shape of a great nulla-nulla, and other shapes that he had not seen before. But as he moved forward again these shapes fell back. Only Ko-in waited at the edge of the dark, with his firestick in his hand making a point of fire, and the white paint on his body catching the light.

He said to Ko-in, 'But I don't know what to do.'

'And there is no teacher and no time. I am no teacher, Clever One. Unwind the cord and look at the power.'

Ko-in might not be a Clever One, but at any rate he was hero. Who else was there to say what Wirrun should do? Reverently he began to unwind the cord.

It was soft and supple, clean and grey under its outer layer, and it came off yard after yard. Wirrun heaped it coil upon coil like a fishing line. The softness diminished and the hardness grew: a small angular hardness with a sharp point to it. At last this core of hardness lay bare in his hand: a single crystal of quartz, perhaps two inches from point to base and an inch across the base. Its hexagonal shape was precise except on one side where it was flawed by an intrusion of stone. It was skeined with pink if the firelight could be trusted, and it had a frosty sparkle. It held rain and sky and dew and frost and the glitter of the sea.

'A very great magic,' said Ko-in softly. 'A magic that reaches across many countries and covers all the land. A magic that reaches to the sky. Wherever the ice may lead you this magic will have power. All the restless things of earth and night will know it in all their countries. They will let you pass, or help you. I have done well, Clever One.'

'No,' said Wirrun, his fingers busy rewinding the cord. 'I'm not Clever. That's the People's business, and there's more to it. But I reckon if you give me this it'll help me, and after it can go back in the cave. I needn't look at it again.' He finished rerolling the cord and hung the power in its net bag on his belt again. 'You never know, it might tell me something. I could do with a bit more telling.'

'Ah,' said Ko-in. 'But now another will tell, I think. Come and listen.'

He moved along the ledge into the dark, and Wirrun followed. A little way behind the end of the ledge and close to the rock behind, Ko-in stopped. The darkness of a tree-trunk rose and disappeared above into the darkness of leaves. In the trunk by Ko-in's head was a patch of deeper blackness, a hole. Ko-in spoke to it.

'Come out, stranger. You who belong in another country far away, say what you do in mine. You know the law: those who come into a country that is not their own should have permission. Come out and speak.'

The silence within the tree was as deep as the dark. Nothing moved there. Nothing breathed. It was such a silence that Wirrun knew something listened and hid inside the tree. Ko-in reached into the hole and gently drew something out, holding it long and limp in his hand.

'Don't be afraid,' he said. 'Yet.'

He led the way back to the fire, and Wirrun at last could see what he held. A dark female figure, taller and more stick-thin than he would have believed possible; wispy arms and legs twisted together; dark possum-eyes wide with fear.

It was the Mimi.

Three

The Mimi's round eyes shone green in the fire-light as she turned her head this way and that. She would have slithered off into the dark, but it billowed and twisted into shapes wherever she looked. The earth-creatures were gathered out of reach of the fire, and they were angry at this intruding spirit. She could not have got far.

She looked at the wall of rock that rose behind Wir-run's camp. She might have tried to slip away into that, but there were worse things in there. Beside her stood Ko-in who was hero, wearing the white paint of the People. He looked stern, but not angry; yet. The other who watched her so curiously was the young man she knew of. It embarrassed and distressed her that he should watch her like that for, though she had half ex-pected it from Wirrun, she was not used to being seen by humans. She turned her eyes away from him, this way and that—and then she stepped close to the fire.

In all her weeks of hiding and fearing the Mimi had not dared to make a fire. That was banishment and iso-lation indeed; for who is the homeless, the outcast of earth, but the one who has lost his right to fire? The Mimi stood drooping by Wirrun's fire with her dark eyes fixed on the coals.

'Come, you must speak,' said Ko-in not too kindly.

'It will be remembered that you did not choose to come to my country. But you come with the ice and the hunter of ice, a rock-spirit nesting in a tree. There are reasons and causes to be told, fibres of knowing to be joined into one cord. Speak.'

'I can't tell—I don't know—I won't say—' whispered the Mimi.

Ko-in towered over her frowning. 'And in my country who gives you the right of can't and don't and won't? Are your ears duller than the ears of one who is not even a proper man? Have you lived your long time listening within rock and you do not yet hear the voice of the land? You are ordered to speak, and not only by me. Tell how you left your own country.'

That the Mimi knew and could tell. 'The wind. It carried me here.'

'Ah well,' said Ko-in with scornful pity. 'The wind is no toy for a straw thing. Those who cannot ride it should stay out of its path.'

At this the Mimi seemed to sneeze. She drew her thin body to its full length, standing almost as tall as Ko-in, and Wirrun saw that the sneeze had really been an indignant snort. The Mimi was offended.

'You are a rider of the wind, old thing, and I am a straw,' she said proudly. 'But I have ridden a tribe of winds and yet I am not broken. You have made your little journeys here and there about your country, but I have ridden over every country across all the land from one sea to another. There has never in all time been such a riding of winds, and I still have my arms and legs.'

In the firelight Wirrun thought that Ko-in's eyes twinkled, but he spoke with grave respect. 'Then indeed we need your skill and wisdom, woman. And did you never rest in all that riding? Did you sleep on the wind?'

The Mimi grew uneasy and drooped. 'There is no sleep on the wind,' she muttered, looking this way and that. 'I rested one night.'

'And did you nest in a tree that night also?' asked Ko-in. 'Are your powers too weak for strange rocks?'

He watched her restless eyes. 'You rested in rock in a western country and saw the ice.' A shiver passed down her long body from head to feet. 'You saw the men of ice in their own country, and then you rode the winds again to mine. And here you rested in a rock for a while, and ate our food; but later, as Ko-in saw, you nested in a tree like a bird or a possum. Yet the ice had not come here then. Why did you fear it so? What did you learn on that one night in the western rocks?'

The Mimi's eyes shone green as she looked at Wirrun. 'He was there,' she said sulkily.

'That night!' cried Wirrun, staring at her.

'He was there,' Ko-in agreed, 'and has told what he knows. But he did not see or hear the men of ice. That is for you to tell. Why did you fear them here in my country when they were still far off?'

'The wind blows,' whispered the Mimi, 'and the ice creaks. And the frost rustles like sand.'

'In the western rocks. But why do they come here?'

The shapes of dark round the firelight pressed in a little. The Mimi shivered.

'They will take the land again,' she whispered. 'They will build the ice and whiten all the land. As it was before.'

Now Wirrun too stirred. He had known it was a terrible ice.

'But this they do not do,' Ko-in said. 'They walk through rocks and peep out at the sea and make a little frost. What do they seek?'

'They seek the one who fought them before with fire, to freeze it and crack its bones. They will find the Nargun, the Eldest of Narguns, first.'

'The Eldest Nargun?' Ko-in seemed astonished. 'That was another battle, long ago. Do they seek that Nargun now? Where do they seek it?'

'In its own country by the sea. In the south, they say.'

'Well . . . we have joined the fibres of knowing into a cord. I thank you, woman. You are free of our rocks when the ice has passed. You are free of our food and no creature will harm you. But you will come when a great one calls.'

The Mimi crouched over the fire. 'Take some,' said Wirrun, and she rolled her dark eyes at him and watched him lay on more wood.

'Come, Clever One,' said Ko-in. Wirrun shrugged at the title and decided not to argue. He thought that Ko-in had chosen to keep to it, and once he had made a choice he would not easily change it. 'It is full night now, and we must talk at my fire where no ears listen. Close your hand on the power.' He held Wirrun tightly round the shoulders and sprang into the air.

This time, with his hand on the power and Ko-in's arm about his shoulders, Wirrun rose upright through the air as a diver rises through water: above the scrub, with his fire a red twinkle below; above the mountain and forward into the wind. The stars welcomed him. The hills spread out their folds for him, wearing the dark draperies of their forests. A river marked its path for him to read. He was laughing, as Ularra sometimes laughed, with the pain of delight, and the wind in his ears fluttered with laughter too. . . . They were dropping between trees to another red twinkle of fire and Wirrun, falling like a stone beside Ko-in, laughed again with the delight of fear. . . . They were down and Wirrun was tumbled beside the fire, his hands still tight on the power, laughing as he fought for breath.

'I thank you,' said Ko-in, sitting there too with a laugh of his own in his eyes. 'It is a very long time since I last felt flight. I had forgotten it with use.'

'Wish I could,' said Wirrun, shaking his stiff fingers. 'That'd be something, forgetting it with use. And I'd stand a lot better chance catching the Ninya. They'll be a day and two nights ahead by the time I get started tomorrow.'

'And youth goes out of your face with the thought.' Ko-in sat silent, brooding. He roused himself and turned again to Wirrun. 'Tell me your plans, Clever One, now that you have the power of the People and have heard the rock-spirit from the north.'

'Well . . .' said Wirrun awkwardly. 'I gotta thank you for all that, and it helps. Only there's not a lot I can do, see. It'll have to be the men with the right songs that send the Ninya back, and I've sent word for 'em to come. But they'll take a time. There'll have to be a lot of talking to get the story straight, and I don't know how they'll travel but it's a long way any rate. All I can do is what I thought before: just hang on till the men come. Follow up these Ninya, and keep letting the men know where they are and what they're up to.'

Ko-in frowned. 'It is you who know the business of the People—but it is not a powerful plan. We fought more mightily once. You have now a great advantage over these men of ice, these Ninya. For they know only that they travel south, and must go by the caverns in the rocks and look always for the sea. But you know what they seek and can go there straight and fast.'

'M'm . . . as long as they don't change their minds and start building ice when I'm five hundred miles ahead.'

'But you have sent word to the right men. If the Ninya start building ice the men will know of it. They will go to the ice. Now think: if the Ninya keep on their path to the Eldest Nargun? You might reach it first, and rouse it to hold them until the men can come.' He frowned again, and seemed puzzled. 'Well, it is good that they seek it, for it keeps them within their caverns and tells you how to track them.'

'What is this thing they're looking for, anyhow? Where's its place?'

'A Nargun? It is a monster of rock. It lives in the south and the People avoid it with fear because from time to time it crushes and eats one of them. Narguns are born from the fire deep in the earth, and because this is the Eldest it has the power of First Things. It can call up fire, and was the worst enemy of the Ninya once.'

'And that's what you want me to rouse? Well . . . I just hope I don't get crushed and eaten.'

Ko-in laughed. 'You do not know your strength,

Clever One. For the land is under you and you have the power of the People.'

'M'm. Well, it should save time knowing where to go. Where's this country?'

'Ah, the countries. Who can tell the People where the countries are? Its name would be strange to you and its People are spread far; but the Eldest Nargun remains. The country is far south, by that coast where the land turns sharply west. You must ask for the Eldest Nargun as you go.'

'But that'll take a time! Finding the People to ask, waiting while they hunt up some old man who still remembers—I won't be much better off than the Ninya! Except I can stick to the coast while they dodge round in caverns.'

'You will be much better off, for you will not look for the People unless you chance to need them. The earth-things will be awake all along your way as they are here, for they sense the ice from far off. They will be as active as wasps, and their memory is longer than the People's; and you have the power at your belt. They must help you. Ask the earth-things.'

'Well . . . all right. *If* I can get ahead of these Ninya, and *if* they're so scared of this Eldest Nargun, and *if* it doesn't crush me and eat me, and *if* the men don't come in time, and *if* the things outside this country know the power . . . A lot of ifs, I reckon.'

Ko-in was looking displeased. 'Mighty battles are fought on ifs,' he said severely. 'You need not fear the Nargun or the earth-things; for I have told you that this power is a very great magic known to all things in this land. I have given you much help and will now give you more. We must return to your fire, for the night deepens and there must be time for sleep. Is your hand on the power?'

They sprang up again through the darkness of trees into the wind and stars. They flew together, youth and hero, an army of two against the ice; and they dropped into the folds of the mountain and down to Wirrun's fire. There Ko-in stared for a moment at the rock-face behind the camp, then turned away from it and raised his voice. It was a strong and ringing voice.

'Rock-spirit of the north, Ko-in calls you. Come and talk again.'

They waited, Wirrun a good deal taken by surprise. Ko-in was about to call again when the Mimi came into the firelight from the direction of her tree.

'So you do not yet trust the rocks, spirit-woman,' Ko-in greeted her.

'Mimi,' she said pettishly. 'I'm a Mimi.'

'Indeed.' Ko-in bowed his head. 'Then you were right. You have come from very far and there has never been such a riding of winds. It needed skill, in one whose greatest enemy is the wind. You have conquered your enemy, woman of the Mimi,' said Ko-in, making one of his pronouncements. The Mimi straightened her drooping shoulders. 'Yet I think you are not able to direct the wind? How will you return?'

She drooped again. 'The right wind will come,' she whispered.

'And carry you over the mountains before it falls. And the wrong one will come again and carry you back here, or over the sea, and drop you again. Will you trust your frail limbs to the dust-devils or the ocean?'

The Mimi shivered and was silent. Wirrun was sorry for her and wondered what Ko-in was about. He was beginning to suspect that Ko-in, hero or not, liked to talk. For one who claimed that the talking was over and the doing should begin he had talked a good deal tonight.

'But perhaps,' he said now, 'you are happy here in my beautiful country. Perhaps you do not wish to return to the country of the monsoons.'

Her eyes shone green as she raised her head, and she gave that snort that was like a cat's sneeze. 'Your country is very well for those who can do no better. It should not be spoken of with my rich and lovely country, my far home . . .' Her voice trailed off, but she summoned it again and hissed at him. 'It will be long before the ice ventures into *my* country.'

Wirrun admired her for speaking so with the creatures of this country rustling and blowing in the dark all around her. 'It's the one land under all of us,' he said quickly, to get in before Ko-in could make an angry reply. But Ko-in did not seem angry with the Mimi and only bowed his head again.

'How will you return?' he repeated. There was no answer. The Mimi drooped. 'Your skill and courage deserve some help,' said Ko-in. 'This one can help you.' He pointed to Wirrun, who stared at him in amazement. So did the Mimi.

'Listen,' said Ko-in. 'This one goes on a journey to serve the land. He must go far and fast, and somewhere along the way there will be winds. With your help and the power of the People he can use the winds. He must talk with earth-spirits on his way, and you will know them better than he. You must travel with him.'

'I won't go,' said the Mimi at once and with force.

'You must go. The land requires it.'

'You are not the land,' hissed the Mimi. 'You do not speak with its voice.'

'But you hear its voice. Listen again. This one goes to find that Nargun that the ice men dread, to call it into battle with them. You will not stay here fighting on the side of the ice.'

'I won't go,' she said again. 'I fight no battles. I am not hero but frail, a hider in the land. I was not meant for battles.'

'Then you must hide in another country, for this one will not hide you.'

Wirrun was angry at Ko-in's cruelty. 'She doesn't have to go,' he snapped; and the Mimi repeated desolately, 'I won't go.'

'What, not to return to your rich and lovely country, your far home?' The round possum-eyes turned quickly to Ko-in, and he went on. 'At the end of his journey this one meets men of the Ninya's country which is near your own. The winds are steadier there, and men travel from that country to yours. If you have helped the People they must help you. They will send you home.'

The Mimi twisted her arms together. 'I won't go,' she said, both helpless and obstinate.

'She can't,' Wirrun agreed. 'I gotta start off through the Happy Folk's towns, and I gotta get started quick. Unless the right wind happens to come straight off, that means I gotta go the first way by train. She can't do that, with all those Happy Folk looking at her.'

'They will not see her,' said Ko-in. 'No man, even of the People, can see a Mimi unless he carries a great power or the land itself gives him eyes. She will travel hidden as if in rock.'

'Well I reckon you're too tough,' Wirrun exploded. 'She doesn't want to go, and I can get on without her. I'd rather.' He looked nervously at the Mimi's frail limbs. 'It'd be like looking after a mayfly.'

Ko-in smiled gently. 'She has lived a thousand ages and ridden the winds across the lands, and still those mayfly limbs are unbroken. I am no monster of the dark, Clever One. She must go, for it is her only way home. She has courage; she will know the spirits; and her eyes and ears are the best in the land. And if the wind is right and you hold the power between you, then both may ride the wind safely.' He turned to the Mimi again. 'Go to your nest and eat and sleep, and come here at first light. This one will find a way for you to travel.'

The Mimi had been stealing glances at Wirrun and listening sharp-eared. 'I won't go,' she said pettishly, and flounced away spring-kneed.

When they had watched her go Ko-in laid his hand on Wirrun's shoulder and smiled again. 'It has been a long day since the ice at dawn, but there is still time for sleep. You will rest well and wake well and journey well out of my country. After that you will listen to the land and the power, and journey well to the end. And I, Ko-in, I will go back to watching alone and silent, and my love will follow you. I will talk to no more People till the ice comes again.' He gripped Wirrun's shoulder tightly. 'I never knew a man who was angry with me three times in one day.'

Then Wirrun dared to put his own hand on Ko-in's shoulder. It felt smooth like stone and hard like leather. 'Not three times, only twice,' he said. 'That Clever One stuff, I just know it's not right. Like my cheek, anyhow, when you've done it all for me. Whatever happens, it'll be good to remember you. And thanks, man—' He stopped, confused. That was no name for Ko-in who was hero.

Ko-in chuckled. 'Goodbye, Man.' Like a diver rising from the ocean he sprang towards the stars and was gone. Wirrun was alone with the mountain in the soft scurry of the night.

Heavy with the need for sleep he glanced over his supplies, packed a few and buried others, laid his gear ready for morning. Then he dragged himself into his sleeping-bag and slept like a stone.

3

❖❖❖❖❖❖❖❖❖❖❖❖❖❖❖❖❖❖❖❖❖❖❖❖❖❖❖❖❖❖❖❖❖❖❖❖❖❖

Wirrun and
the Mimi

One

Wirrun woke at dawn, and in the first moment of knowing it seemed to him that the mountain held him: that this place, this one spot, was home. He sat up feeling sad and comforted in the same moment; for today he must leave the mountain, yet this spot would always be here. And as he sat up he saw the Mimi.

She was sitting by his fireplace staring at the charred remains of his fire. Her stick-like knees were drawn up, and a cloud of wispy hair fell around her large ears to hide her face. It was the first time he had seen her by day and he sat quiet for a moment to look. It was like seeing the half-imagined shapes of night take on the reality of day.

He had seen Ko-in by day and had flown with him; but Ko-in was hero, not earth-thing. As the mountain had bred its shadowy creatures so man through long ages had bred Ko-in: not as mystic as the sky but larger than life; not man but of man, sharing his better self. Ko-in was real enough to be seen by day. To see the Mimi sitting by his fire was to see some darker, secret, older being out of night or the earth. From what Ko-in had said he must get used to such things.

He felt her peeping at him through her hair, so he stopped looking and spoke. 'What's up? Can't you make a fire?'

She hissed at him. 'Only a fool makes a fire in a strange country.'

'That's me,' said Wirrun cheerfully. He climbed fully dressed out of his sleeping-bag and began to make the fire. 'Want something to eat?'

She shook her head, and he wanted her to stop in case her fragile neck broke. While he ate his quick breakfast he remembered Ko-in's confident promise: 'This one will find a way for you to travel.' He had no idea how she should travel.

'You can't walk, I reckon,' he muttered, looking at her critically over a slice of toast. 'Your legs wouldn't stand it for one thing, and there's the wind for another.'

She said nothing. Well, if she couldn't walk she had to be carried, that was all.

'Tell you what,' he said suddenly. 'If you live in rocks you must like the dark and you don't care much about air. I can roll you up inside my sleeping-bag and carry you that way.' And he brought the bag, rolled it up and strapped it, unrolled it again and showed her how soft it was. 'Of course,' he added, 'you'd have to curl up a bit, but that ought to be easy.' He had realized that the Mimi was a little taller than he.

'I won't go,' she said scornfully. He was not sure whether she was rejecting the sleeping-bag or the idea of being carried or the whole journey.

'Well,' he said, exasperated, 'if I'm not supposed to carry you I don't know what I'm supposed to do. There's the train, for one thing. I don't suppose you've ever seen one—noisy as hell and they go like the wind. You'd be scared stiff.'

'I go my own way,' said the Mimi.

'You do that,' said Wirrun because he had no more ideas. He watched her rise and walk to the rock wall. She blew, there was a gape of darkness, she was gone.

'That's that, then, and good riddance,' grumbled Wirrun. One part of Ko-in's plan had come unstuck already and it wasn't his fault. He had always thought that the whole plan was full of ifs. At least it meant that the rocks inside the mountain were unfrozen and safe again. And that meant that the Ninya were well away.

'She would've been handy, at that,' he told himself. 'Like a sort of thermometer; you'd know if the ice was close.' He packed his gear, buried his fire, and took up his pack.

The eastern sky was a cloth of gold promising the sun. He set off down the mountain, and it was like leaving some very old person who had been part of his childhood. He stopped now and then on his way down to look back and up. He had done this two or three times when a sort of wink at the edge of his vision made him turn that way and look.

There was nothing.

He turned back and went on down the mountain. There were many things on it that might follow him, and perhaps they were invisible by day; but Ko-in had promised him safe journey out of that country. He laid his hand for a moment on the power at his belt.

He came out of the forest and on to the dusty road he had followed in. Now he could see all round in the open country; nothing followed him. There was not even an Inlander in sight, and only a few cattle grazed in a paddock to his right. Now too he could lengthen his stride to the long, easy lope that he liked. The road began to wind away behind him.

It was like a holiday. Nothing weighed on Wirrun just now, or called to him through his feet; the challenges were all behind or ahead. On this fresh morning of new sun and high white clouds and light winds, he need only enjoy walking until he reached the town. He began to whistle softly.

The road ran under a bank of rocks and tall grass; and as Wirrun walked under the bank a rock winked at him.

He stopped whistling.

Half a mile farther on another rock winked.

Wirrun began to whistle again thoughtfully. What would happen, he wondered, when the ridges lowered and the valley widened? He thought there were miles to come with no rock outcrops near the road; and at the end of those miles there was the town.

Another rock winked. A spark of mischief made Wirrun break into a jog for half a mile. That was foolish when he had so far to go, and at the end of it he sat on a low bank under a grey gum to rest. He had been sitting there for two minutes when the grass rustled as if a lizard moved, and the Mimi stood over him.

He grinned at her. She hunched her narrow shoulders and folded herself down against the gum, sitting with one arm looped around the trunk.

'It is foolish to go so fast,' she said severely. 'The rocks do not know your road. To follow I must always watch; and to watch I must find the points of rock that rise above the ground. It takes time.'

'It's too slow, then,' said Wirrun. 'And you'll wear yourself out. You'd be better off being carried inside my pack.'

The Mimi cat-sneezed at him. 'I am not a dead bush-rat or a twist of cord to be carried on your shoulders. I have ridden the winds.'

Wirrun was about to answer when the sound of a motor made him turn his head quickly. 'Someone's coming,' he warned the Mimi. 'That's a truck.'

'I'm not deaf,' she retorted. 'That sound is heard in my country too. It will pass, for the tree will keep it off; and it travels too slowly to make a wind.'

'There'll be someone driving it, an Inlander. Do you want to be seen?'

But the Mimi sat calmly where she was as the truck came round a bend trailing its dust. It was the truck that brought the newspapers to the village under the mountain. The driver looked closely at Wirrun with hard Inlander eyes, noting his pack and everything about him. Wirrun knew that he would tell them in the village that the Abo who'd been hanging round had moved on all right. Yet in spite of his close inspection the driver took no notice of the Mimi.

'You were told that I am not seen by men,' she said as the truck passed. Then she turned her dark round eyes on Wirrun accusingly. '*You*—' she said, and stopped.

'Sorry,' said Wirrun. 'I can't help it.' It was hard to realize, in spite of telling, that she was invisible to other people when she was so clear to him. 'Look,' he said, 'if they can't see you and you're going to walk anyhow, why can't you walk on the road with me? It'd be a lot shorter and easier for you and we'd make better time.'

'And the wind?' said the Mimi.

'Oh . . . yeah, the wind. Well, why can't I hold your hand?' He looked uneasily at the stick-thin fingers, but he had to get used to them.

'And has the wind spoken to you?—will it be a small wind all the way? Or will it leap with a sudden pull to break off my hand and carry me over the sea?'

'Cripes!' said Wirrun. 'There's got to be a way, though. Because when this little road runs into the big one there won't be any more rocks for you to peep through. So you won't be able to follow.' He closed his hand on the power at his belt as he thought of the problem. Suddenly his fingers were throbbing and he knew what to do. He unfastened his belt and slipped off the net bag. 'Look,' he said. 'This is the way.'

He unwound a yard or so of the soft fur cord and tied it under the next winding so that it would unroll no further. Then he tied the free end into a long loop and passed it through the mesh of the bag so that it hung outside.

'Now,' he said, 'you can hang on to that while you're walking. We won't both be holding the power, just you, so we won't go flying off on the wrong wind. Only the wind won't take you while you've got a line to the power. Try it and see.'

He could see that the Mimi did not favour the idea. Her dark eyes were fixed on the distant hills. 'I am not a dog to be tied to your belt,' she said coldly. 'You speak of speed; we do not make it by sitting still.' She extended herself upward, sighted along the line of the road, then mounted its bank like a very tall stick-insect and blew on a boulder that looked only big enough to sit on. Wirrun saw it gape darkly; the Mimi slid into it feet first, and the rock winked closed.

'Cantankerous female,' he muttered crossly, picking up his pack and setting off again. If she wanted to make her own way she could; he wouldn't be watching for winking rocks or trying to adapt his pace to hers. He trudged on.

The road ran out of the hills into the valley, and by late afternoon he could see the highway ahead. He could hear it, too: an animal moan, rising and dying but never silent. He was nearing the small railway town by now; and suddenly he decided to camp for the night here on the river. It was better than close to the town. If he went on he might catch a train and reach the city by night; but then he would have to spend a night in the city. It would be expensive, it would not save much time, and he didn't like the idea of it. As for the Mimi, he had no idea how she was going to manage in any case and was certain that he didn't care; for himself, he would camp by the river, sleep and wake early, and reach the town in time for the first trains. He could reach the end of the short southern line in one day, leaving all the city area and the Happy Folk behind.

At a point where the road was out of sight of houses or farm buildings he climbed through a fence and made for the river. Following it along a little way he found a shelving bank overhung by river oaks. There were no grazing cattle to bring a horseman; in fact milking was probably over already. He unrolled his pack on the shelf of the bank. Below it, on the coarse river sand, he laid a few stones for a fire-place and set his fire ready. It was still too early and too warm to eat. He left the fire unlit and went to lie on his sleeping-bag and rest. It had been a long day, and tomorrow would start early.

He lay listening to the quiet talk of the river, and the wind singing softly in the needles of the oaks. It was the first chance he had had to think quietly over the plans Ko-in had made for him. There was a lot to think about, for Ko-in and his help had changed Wirrun's course completely. He was no longer simply a scout for the men of Mount Conner. He was now an advance party, to harass and hold the ice till the men arrived; and his journey was a race against the Ninya, who must already be far to the south. Wirrun hoped he might overtake them in his day's journey by train, but there was something else to be thought about before that. He must send fresh word to the men.

What word should he send? That the Ninya were headed for some unknown point near 'the coast where the land turns sharply west'? Not very easy to explain in a telegram—or even if you were talking to them. Should he arrange to meet them at some more precise point, say on the Victorian border? But the Ninya might change their plans and begin to build the ice before they reached it. It would be better, as Ko-in had said, to let the men follow the frosts. Yet he needed to send them some message of the Ninya's doings and his own. He worked it out and wrote it in pencil on the margin of one of his maps: 'Going south fast big ice coming send men quick.' That was the best he could do; and he only hoped the men really would be quick for he didn't like the sound of this Nargun, the Eldest with the power of fire.

He did not even know from what direction the men would come, or how they would travel the long and lonely miles. Not by plane, he thought; even if they had the money, they would not like to be carried on tribal business by the Happy Folk. But the People had their own ways of cutting a knotty problem; and all along those miles there would be others, a scattered few of the People here and there, to know the fastest route and help them on their way. They would come. And thinking this Wirrun fell into a doze.

The wind was still hushing in the oaks when he woke, and the river was talking louder. There was soft light from a young moon that would soon be setting, and the red-yellow light of his fire. . . . But he had not lit his fire. And what was that smell of cooking? He sat up and looked over the bank to the sand below.

The Mimi was sitting over the fire eating a fat, fire-blackened root. As Wirrun watched she reached out with a stick and dragged another from the coals. It looked to him like a good big sweet-potato from a farm garden. It lay cooling while she went on hungrily stuffing the first into her mouth; but even while she did this she stared absorbed at the fire. Wirrun stood up, stretched, and came slowly down the bank.

'Good fire,' he said. 'You're always catching me asleep.'

She blinked up at him like a possum, dragged another root from the coals, picked up the second and broke it open, and went back to staring at the fire. Wirrun set a tin of stew to heat. His supplies were running low; he would have to buy more tomorrow. Sniffing the good smell of roasting, he thought he would have preferred one of the Mimi's stolen roots.

They ate together in silence while the moon set and the fire grew redder. Afterwards Wirrun tidied his camp: flattening and burying the empty tin, filling his waterbag for tomorrow, washing his plate and himself in the river. The Mimi began by watching curiously, but at some point while Wirrun was busy she vanished.

He was not at all surprised. He sat and watched the fire go out and held the power between his hands, feeling again its completeness and strength; and he thought of the mountain, and of the dark things and Ko-in, and then of the Ninya and the Eldest Nargun; and now and then anxiously of the train.

When the moon and the fire were both out he went to sleep under the whispering river-oaks and slept to the talking of the water till earliest dawn. He breakfasted without a fire, rolled his pack, and climbed out of the river. By sunrise he had reached the highway and made some distance along it, forging ahead on its wide verge.

It was a little after sunrise when something flickered at the edge of his vision and something flicked at his belt. The Mimi was walking beside him, holding to the possum-fur cord.

Two

'Nice morning,' said Wirrun.

'From here the rock goes only down,' muttered the Mimi sulkily.

It was a moment to talk about something else but difficult to know what to say. It was pleasing to have won a battle with the Mimi, but it meant that the worrying problem of the train was his alone to solve. And he could not help feeling ridiculous with this tall, frail figure walking jerk-kneed at his side and clinging to a cord from his belt.

He said, "Yeah, well, we'll be in the town soon. You won't like it—I'm sorry about that—but we've got to get through a lot of it to get to the coast in the south. It'll take all day, even in the train, but we'll be right by tonight. The train takes us through fast, just like riding the wind again. Only this time you'll be inside where there's no wind, sitting pretty on a soft seat.'

He glanced sideways. She was looking obstinate again, staring ahead and saying nothing. It was no good. However he might try to encourage them both, in no way could he picture the Mimi travelling by train.

Several cars howled past, and both Wirrun and the Mimi cringed. She had clutched at the possum-fur cord in fear of the sudden wind; he had watched under his heavy brow for a sign of turning heads and pointing fingers. Neither happened: no jerk at his waist and no curious eyes. They glanced sideways at each other, each proved right and each a little smug. Wirrun thought of something he had wanted to ask her last night.

'If you can follow me through the rocks, couldn't you go home that way?'

'Do you not know the law?' she said. 'How many countries lie between me and mine? All with their rock-spirits, angry at strangers. How can I go so far alone in strange rocks full of fear and trouble?'

'The Ninya seem to manage.'

She shivered. 'They send their wind ahead, freezing the way as they go. Who could stand against the ice? But I: I am frail and a hider. I do no harm and nothing fears me. Even the People do not fear me.'

'Don't let it worry you,' said Wirrun. 'You rode the winds, didn't you? You've seen all across the land, and now you're seeing a town, and you're going south and helping to fight the ice. They ought to pin a medal on you.'

The Mimi raised her head and looked fiercely at the town which they were now entering. But she walked very close to Wirrun and he thought it was lucky that her first town was a small one. He could not help feeling strange himself. He was glad that it was still very early and so few people were about. None of them gave him more than a glance or seemed to notice even the cord looping outward from his belt. Their faces showed that they all had something important to do and were grimly intent upon doing it. Wirrun suddenly felt that it would not have mattered if they had seen the stick-figure springing along at his side. Some, knowing no word for it, would not have believed what they saw; others would have run in fear from the frail hider.

'I'd rather have you than any of this lot,' he grumbled to the Mimi; and she cat-sneezed in anger because the comparison was an insult.

'Never mind, their trains are fast. The station's round this corner.'

He led the Mimi on to it. If they couldn't see her she wouldn't need a ticket; he bought one, for as far south as the coast line went, and asked about timetables and changes. While he was doing this an express roared through, and he felt the Mimi stiffen and quiver at his side. There was going to be trouble all right.

'What was that?' she hissed as he turned away from the window. He didn't answer until he had led her down to the end of the platform where he could talk quietly.

'That was a sort of a train,' he said then, 'but we're not getting in one like that. We'll just stand here and watch a couple so you can have a look at 'em, and then we'll get in a nice quiet one.'

'I won't go,' said the Mimi. She was clutching the cord in both hands, looking desperately up and down the line and at the rough vacant land opposite. Wirrun didn't blame her. When you really looked at it, a train was a rude and noisy fuss to make about getting from one place to another.

A second train drew in and stopped. The Mimi cringed, twisting her head from side to side as she tried to hide her ears. Wirrun talked soothingly.

'The noise is only on the outside, that and the wind. Look there—see the people sitting inside, quiet as quiet? There's seats, see? Trains don't hurt you, they—' the train whined out of the station and roared off down the line '—get you a long way fast,' said Wirrun winningly.

'I won't go,' said the Mimi. She let go the cord, sprang long-legged down to the line and across it, leapt over a fence, and dived into a tangle of blackberry.

Wirrun groaned. 'Now she'd done it—she'll never get out of that! She'll be tangled up and broken into matches.' He turned to run off the station, heard another train coming and hesitated. He couldn't cross the line till the train had passed, and the Mimi was not going to wait for him; the damage would be done. And he had to keep things straight: what had to be done was to start his race against the ice. He wasn't supposed to risk that by being a broody hen to a Mimi. She would have to take her chance. At the back of his mind he had always known that she couldn't travel by train.

The train drew in at his platform and Wirrun stepped

doggedly on board. At least he hadn't wasted money buying a ticket for her. The train whined out of the station and hurled itself south, beating its song-sticks and howling its song; and Wirrun stared moodily out of the window.

The Mimi had been an irritating companion, all fears and prickly pride, hating this journey, resenting Wirrun because he was a man but could see her. Yet he wished sadly that he could have helped her safely home. She wasn't far from the coast where there were plenty of rocks; but even if she could disentangle herself unbroken from the blackberry there was nothing on the way to protect her from the wind.

'I never shoulda come by train,' he told himself. 'I knew she couldn't do it.' But what choice had there been? It was his one chance of catching up with the Ninya.

He stared at the Happy Folk who shared the carriage with him. There were not many of them yet, but they all looked as though they had something important to do and must do it at any cost. Well, so had he; the thought became a weight of anxiety. The small towns grew bigger, joined hands and became one; passengers boarded and left; Wirrun no longer saw any of them. He was seeing the men of Mount Conner receiving his message.

There would be a lot of talk and argument before they decided to act. After that they would talk and argue again about who, and how many, should go. Then they would have to raise some money for the trip, and probably round up a couple of cars or trucks. These would be old, and would break down often on the way. Would they take the good road that was so much longer, south then east and north? Or would they risk the shorter road east? In either case it would be a dangerous and terrible journey. For the first time Wirrun felt that the men could not possibly arrive in time. There was only Wirrun. He must win this race. He must force the Eldest Nargun into battle.

The train reached the city and he had to change to

another. Between trains he must find a post office and send his message to Ularra, and he must spend more of his scarce money to buy supplies. Hurry, hurry. . . . He bought a newspaper too, and caught his second train. This one was full to begin with and would empty along the way. It was hard to find room for himself and his pack, but he found a seat at last and opened the paper.

There was no time for thoughtful reading when the whole land and all these busy people depended on Wirrun's speed. He skimmed quickly through for news of the Ninya. There were no new stories of frost but several letters about the earlier stories, an article by a meteorologist, and another by a psychologist. Wirrun had to read them all in case they mentioned some report that he had missed since his last paper. The letters suggested that the frosts were caused by rays from a neighbouring planet, or by a crack in the field of gravity, or by vested interests, and that in any case it was time they were stopped. The meteorologist claimed that the frosts had simply not occurred at all but if they had they must be blamed on something called a Black Spot. The psychologist explained about crowd psychology and the effect of unexpected weather on the emotionally insecure. Several of them mentioned specific areas of frost and Wirrun, after careful checking, decided that he had missed no new reports. He still had no idea how far the Ninya had travelled now.

He tried to calculate their speed, going over in his mind the frosts he knew about and the days between. It seemed that the Ninya had varied their speed very widely, travelling sometimes only about twelve miles in a day and sometimes very much more. The fastest must have been from their own country to the east; at best he had to allow about eighty miles in a day for that stretch. Of course he did not know how far each stretch had been, how the caverns might wind to and fro deep down in the rock, how they might have to find their way from one level to another; but it worried him to know how quickly they could sometimes travel. What hope could he have, with perhaps three hundred miles to travel on foot? One day's journey by train was not enough—he should have scraped up the money from somewhere to hire a plane, or at least a car. If only this line went a bit further south!

So Wirrun's thoughts went round and round, and his body tightened into a knot of worry, while the train rushed south beside the sea. The passengers thinned, the towns dropped hands and drew apart. There were green hills, steep but humped with age, and below the scarp lay the sea. The sun crawled down low behind the hills, and the train drew in to the small town at the end of the line. Wirrun got out, leaving his newspaper behind on the seat as the Happy Folk liked to do. They sometimes talked about tidy trains, but if they had wanted them there would have been garbage containers in the trains.

It was late to start walking, but he needed to start. He needed a quiet camping place out of town, and much more than that he needed to feel he had started on his slow race. He took out the right map, shouldered his pack, and began to walk.

He left behind the railway towns and the highway, and found his way by lonelier roads to the sea. When the first stars came out he was striding south, with the yellow lights of a village winking open and the sea endlessly mourning away to the left. By then he knew that all day the train and the Happy Folk had been fooling him. He had come to them too soon from the quiet of the mountain, and some of their frenzy had got into him.

He knew again that the men from Mount Conner would come, and that all across the land the People would help them. He knew that the speed of the Ninya was all a matter of guessing and for his part he could only do what he must. He could not have run his race with them in a plane or car or train like a can of peaches on wheels, for he knew only roughly where the country of the Narguns was and not at all where the El-dest could be found. He had to find out from the earth-

things as he went. The men could travel after him
as fast as they might, but he must find their path; and
to do that he must walk the land in its quiet places and
trust to it. All he knew so far he had learnt in this way.
It was the only way.

He left the track to join a fellowship of banksias and
laid down his pack among them. In the day's last light
he built his fire and enjoyed the first night's luxury of
grilling chops. The dark came down with a sense of
companionship in it. He lifted his eyes from the chops
and saw the Mimi again, sitting at the edge of the firelight and eating a lizard with her round dark eyes fixed
on the fire.

Three

When Wirrun saw the Mimi he was filled with a
sudden delight. It astonished him, but he was careful
not to let it show too much. He was sure she would only
have hissed or snorted.

'Why don't you come near the fire?' he said. 'Don't
you want to roast your lizard?' He took a stick and
dragged a few coals to the edge of the fire.

The Mimi looked from the fire, to Wirrun, to the
lizard. She had only begun eating the tail. She shuffled
closer, laid the lizard on the coals, and used another
stick to cover it with ashes and more coals. Wirrun
smiled with content. She might be frail and full of fear
and prickly pride, but she had kept her bargain with
Ko-in in spite of it; and she had trusted Wirrun to send
her safely home.

He forked his chops from the fire and offered her
one. She ignored it, dragged out the lizard, and began

to peel back the skin. Wirrun drew a little water from his canvas bag into a mug and set it near her.

'How did you find me?' he asked.

'I looked for fire in a strange country,' she said, and he wondered if she could possibly be teasing.

'But how did you get down here at all?'

'You said south, and by the coast. There are rocks all the way.'

'But how did you get to 'em out of that blackberry? I thought you'd get caught up in it and break yourself for sure.'

She hissed at him angrily. 'I am not a fool. I can find my way through a bramble; and behind it I saw the rock.'

'You fooled me, then; only how did you know how far the train was coming?'

'That noise—how could I lose it? The rocks shook with it; even the rock-spirits of this place have been driven off. When there was no more shaking I began to look for a fire.'

Wirrun shook his head with admiration. 'I don't know why I worry about you,' he said.

The Mimi looked at him for a moment, then drank a little water from the mug. They finished their separate meals, but Wirrun put off the jobs of tidying up. If he turned his back she would vanish into some hiding place, and after that day in the train he wanted her by his fire a little longer. Its flames flickered and sank, and a little way off the sea poured and poured.

'You know what we gotta do?' asked Wirrun.

She answered promptly. 'I help you speak to the spirits, and ride the wind when it is east of north. At the end you find a way for me to travel home. *Not*,' she added, 'rolled up like a cord in a rug.'

'Well, if you'd rather ride the wind home without the power to help you—'

She hissed again. Wirrun saw that if teasing was allowed it must be on one side only and he would have to make it up to her.

'Only it's not just me you're helping,' he said. 'You're

doing it to fight the ice, and I don't know how I'd get on without you.' He wondered if that was a bit too much, if she would see through it and cat-sneeze at him; but she only looked a little queenly. 'I been worried all day,' he added.

The Mimi drank another drop of water.

'Wish I knew where these Ninya are now,' Wirrun murmured as if he were talking to himself. 'We've gotta get ahead of 'em and be first to find this Eldest Nargun. And for all Ko-in says, we haven't got much idea where to look.' He waited for her to shrug, or to give some sign that this was not her affair, but she went on brooding over the fire and he hoped she might be listening. So he went on.

'Just have to keep our eyes peeled for signs of the ice and our ears open for news. Well, you've got the best eyes and ears in the land, and I've got the power. If we stick together and the right winds come we might manage all right.'

'I go my own way,' said the Mimi.

To hide a grin Wirrun reached for fresh wood for the fire. When he turned back she had gone again. He was vexed, for he had wanted to suggest that they travel mostly by night. It was the best time for the earth and earth-things, and the easiest way to avoid the Happy Folk. But he knew now that there would soon be another chance to talk to the Mimi, and tonight at least he needed rest. So, probably, did she. He tidied his camp, banked down the fire, took off his shirt and shorts, and went to bed. His belt with the power fastened to it he took into the sleeping-bag with him. Funny how he hadn't thought of it once while he sat in the train. . . .

. . . Something, a grass-stem or a spider, was tickling his face. He brushed it off and turned over to sleep again. . . . Something fluttered about his neck, and a voice was calling. He sat up quickly and opened his eyes. It was dark, but the dawn was coming.

'Wake up, wake up!' the voice was crying. 'Stupid—log—' A twig of leaves fluttered in his face with a twig of fingers at the end of it.

'I *am* awake,' said Wirrun crossly. 'It's you.' He peered into the paling dark. As his eyes gave up sleep he could see the Mimi herself. She was wound around the trunk of a banksia, reaching out a long skinny arm to brush at Wirrun with the leaves.

'Get up quickly!' she cried. 'The right wind is coming! Am I to be carried off because a man sleeps like a log?'

'I'm coming, I'm coming,' growled Wirrun, climbing out of his sleeping-bag and reaching for shirt and shorts. 'Have you had breakfast?'

She hissed fiercely. 'Oh yes, you will race the ice, if only it will wait for you to eat. Do you think the wind comes east of north whenever you call for it?'

'All *right*. Quit nagging.' Wirrun buckled the power about his waist and bundled his gear together. The banksia leaves rattled and a sigh of wind breathed down his neck. He felt nervous. It was one thing to be seized and carried strongly aloft by Ko-in. It was quite another to trust himself to the wind and the fragile Mimi. And had Ko-in allowed for the weight of his pack? He slung it from his shoulder and closed his hand on the power, standing like that for a moment to get the feel of it. Its old strength flowed into him, and he held out the loop of cord to the Mimi.

'Can we hold it like this? Or will I take it off the belt?'

'A man would let it fall, and we should both be lost. There is no need.' She took the cord. 'Keep your hand on the power and never take it off. Now walk from under the trees, and when the wind comes strong run with me.'

They walked into grey daylight with the wind blowing lightly in their faces. Whenever it strengthened the Mimi tensed and gripped the cord anxiously. Wirrun saw that the wind was a greater terror for her than for him, yet she faced it without faltering. He ventured to say, 'Are you sure it's the right wind? Feels too far east to me.'

'Up there it is the right wind,' she said shortly. 'A wind is not the same all through.—Come now!'

She began a long-legged lope, bobbing a little between strides like a balloon on a string. Wirrun had to race to keep beside her. The wind curled a hand around him and swung him up like a leaf—the Mimi was bobbing on the cord at arm's length above. Wirrun felt himself tumbled in waves and acted as he would have done in the sea, except that his hand was glued to the power. His eyes were tight shut and for a moment he and the Mimi floundered together. The wind seemed suddenly to lose force—they must have failed—he opened his eyes to see.

They were treading water high above the trees, two swimmers in sunlight with the old land brooding darkly below. The wind carried them gently because now they were floating with it. The shadowed land slipped away beneath, with sometimes a higher hilltop gilded in sun. The Mimi clutched at her cord and her big eyes were solemnly amazed; Wirrun could only guess what the wind had been like when she rode it before. He felt it push at his back with a large hand and laughed as he was hurried forward. The Mimi rolled her eyes towards him and turned them away to the left.

To the left was the wrinkled, silken sea which the Mimi watched in fear. Wirrun watched it too, both for pleasure and to be sure that the wind was a right wind. The coast curved in and they were carried directly over a bay. Seagulls glided with them, wind-ruffled and sun-dazzling, and swung off with loud cries and a beating of wings. Wirrun laughed again: he and the sea were both dreaming. He thought he was flying with seagulls and the sea moved like a dreamer. With slow, slow, power its white waves swung in to the beach; the lace of foam behind them was shaped like movement and yet was still. At the end of the bay where the rocks reached out the sea smashed into them slowly like a dreaming giant. Slow fountains of spray hung poised in the air.

Then they were over land again, with low green hills mimicking the sea and the black line of the highway appearing and disappearing through toy forests. It was netted to the coast by smaller tracks, and the wind washed over them all like water.

All that day they rode the wind along the curving coast, sometimes dropping low and sometimes carried high, and the old land brooded below. They hardly spoke; they had no need, and the wind fluttered in their ears and tore their words away. But Wirrun often laughed, turning his head to the Mimi, and she often watched him curiously. They passed over villages and towns, and from the blue-glass sky watched tiny cars and trucks fussing along like beetles. Wirrun laughed at those too, for they nearly always fell behind. The wind was faster.

Late in the afternoon the wind began to tire, taking them slower and lower then pushing them on and up with an extra effort. And it swung more to the east, so that the beaches disappeared and the sea was a field of stretched silk beyond a fringe of trees. A pair of wicked currawongs darted down at them, clacked their beaks and flew off. Wirrun had begun to fear that they were being carried too far inland when the Mimi called some words that he caught as they were blown away: 'Soon we will fall off the wind.'

He began to think about landing. Did they have any choice of where and when? There were hills ahead, smooth and green below a crown of trees but patched with surfaces of ancient weathered granite here and there. They were beautiful surfaces, moulded into the shapes of the hills rather than rising from them: the hills' own faces looking out from grass and forest. Wirrun thought that if they could reach those hills the hilltops might not be very far below—unless the wind flowed upward over them. He did not want to be carried farther from the coast than this. But the hills were coming closer and he did not know how to get off the wind.

The panic of the morning came back—why hadn't Ko-in told him how to land? He tried to steady himself and let his mind flow into his fingers, but he could only feel their aching. Both his hands were aching, for they had taken turns at gripping the power all day since dawn. Well, there could be only two ways to land: either to keep on holding the power or to let it go. If you did the first you must leave it to the wind to put you down where it chose. If you did the second you must fall; but you could grip the power again at the last moment and break the fall, couldn't you?

He shouted to the Mimi: 'Get ready to land!' At once she twisted herself into a complex knot of arms and legs.

The hills were very close now. He thought and hoped that at the level to which he and the Mimi had now fallen they should strike the central slope of the nearest hill. He could see it clearly ahead: a slope of grass, a surface of granite, a rounded boulder or two. Any minute now—

And then the wind surged upward in a wave, lifting them higher, hurrying them forward. There were trees rushing at them. Wirrun snatched his hand from the power.

The wind screamed upward past his ears—he was a falling stone, dragging the Mimi after him—in panic he clutched the power again. His feet were knocked backward—he was on his knees, and then on his face, on the grass. With a light bump the Mimi fell on top of him.

He lay still for a moment, breathing hard. He didn't seem to be hurt. His mind was saying over and over, 'There must be some other way.' He thought of the Mimi and rolled over quickly: funny, he felt stone-heavy, and the ground was rushing at him as if he were still on the wind. His stomach felt like a balloon that was trying to get away. He looked for the Mimi gasping, 'Are you all right?'

She was sitting stiff and erect beside him, still grasping her loop of cord in case the wind pounced, and gazing far off at the view. When he spoke she turned her dark eyes on him as though he might be a toadstool and probably poisonous. Then she looked back at the view. It was clear that she was too offended to speak. Wirrun ran his eyes quickly over her: four stick-like limbs still there, each with its twigs of fingers and toes.

'Sorry,' he said between breaths. 'Didn't know—first try—better next time—'

She gave him the same glance and looked away again. After a moment she spoke.

'Those who do not know would do well to ask.' She lifted her chin even higher and looked at the sky. 'Those who claim to care for the frail should not hurl the frail to the ground from a great height. It is well that I have learnt to save my own limbs.'

Wirrun sat up, blinking and shaking his head at the view which still seemed to be blowing past him.

'Aw, come on,' he coaxed. 'It wasn't a *great* height. That's why we had to come down fast before we cleared the hill. And I couldn't ask—there wasn't anyone to ask.'

If it had been possible for the Mimi to swell he could see that she would have done so. Instead she hissed. 'Why then,' she demanded, 'did the spirit of the mountain send me to help you ride the wind?'

'Well, sure you helped,' said Wirrun quickly. 'But this was using the power, and you don't know about that. It doesn't even come from your country.'

'And did not the spirit tell you that all creatures in all countries know that power? It is of the sky and I am of the earth, but still I am spirit. How should a man know what a spirit knows? I could have told you to loose your hand only a little and tighten it again at once. We should have climbed down from the wind step by step, not hurtling like spears of lightning.'

Wirrun was obstinately silent, staring at the view and forcing it to keep still. The sun was behind the hill and its long shadow lay in front of him. He told himself that he had had about enough of this; Ko-in had put the power of the People in his hands, not in the Mimi's. Sure he was glad to have her around, but he was getting sick of being bossed by a bundle of sticks. Look at her now, hanging on to her cord like a little kid because she couldn't even stand on her own feet in a breeze.

The shadow of the hill reached further. He could feel the strength and thrust of it, the power of the land itself lifting and holding him.

Let children fight over toys, said the surging hill. *Serve only me, for the ice is coming.*

'All right,' said Wirrun, 'next time I'll ask. Come on, Mimi, I said I was sorry. We'll go across to that rock so you can let go of the cord, and we'll make a fire and have a meal and a bit of a sleep. Then we'll go on while it's still night. That's the best time for us.'

The Mimi gave a righteous sniff and stood up long and thin and severe, like a schoolmarm receiving an apology from the class. Wirrun strode beside her up the slope to a broad bare face of granite that brooded under the hill's crown of trees. They walked across the granite till its grey brow bulged over them; and under this Wirrun took off his pack and laid it on the stone. The Mimi dropped her cord and crouched on the rock.

The slopes below were dusted with purple and the forest rose gold-edged against the setting sun. Wirrun went into it and gathered sticks. The granite was already a safe fireplace. He built the fire's foundation of sticks and went into the forest again for heavier wood. When he brought it back the Mimi had lit the fire and was feeding its flames with bigger sticks.

Even crouched over a fire and on this broad face of rock, she seemed uneasy. She looked from side to side at the purpling shadows. Wirrun wondered if she sensed any coldness in the rocks, or if she could find nothing to eat in this place. If she were half as hungry as he was she might even share his can of meatballs.

A little way from the fire he stooped to lay his wood in a neat pile on the rock. Behind him the Mimi hissed fiercely. He turned his head just in time to see her blow on the rock and vanish into it. Then something struck him hard on the temple and he fell forward over his wood heap.

4

The Ninya

One

Pain thumped and banged in Wirrun's head; he turned it restlessly and felt rock. The thumping came into his head from the rock—it was noise, not pain. There were grunts, too. All around, near and far, a chorus of grunts coming and going: a herd of animals grunting and stomping on rock? He was being tugged and torn—he opened his eyes—closed them again—opened them quickly and tried to sit up.

He was pushed down hard. He struggled against little arms that pushed and tore. No good. They were strong. Strong and hard as iron. A little dark man stood over him brandishing a heavy lump of wood.

A crowd of little dark people swarmed over the rock. They were only about eighteen inches high, but three of them held him easily while they tore at his clothes. They had torn his shirt right off. Others were beating out his fire, thumping and banging at it with sticks. Another hurled his neat pile of firewood piece by piece into the forest. They swarmed like ants and grunted to each other as they worked.

Wirrun fought with the little men near him, but two of them grabbed his arms and legs and dragged him to the edge of the granite. Little iron-hard hands tore at his shorts. Through his shock and daze Wirrun felt a throbbing at his belt. The power—they would take it! He fumbled for the net bag and closed his hand on it just in time. He felt wiry little fingers fastened on the bag. He heaved his shoulders, jabbed with his elbows, and glared into dark angry little faces.

'Hands off!' rumbled Wirrun.

The power was throbbing in his hand. The small wiry fingers fell away. An arm waved; there was quick grunting, then silence. The silence spread. The thumping stopped. They were looking at him from hard dark eyes under heavy brows. Dark-eyed and heavy-browed, Wirrun stared back.

There were one or two grunts, and this time Wirrun thought they held words. 'Back,' he thought he had heard, and, 'Ants.' The hands seized him again and he made ready to fight, but this time they dragged him back up the rock and set him against its bulging brow. One of them dropped his shirt beside him. Then they squatted at a little distance and stared at him again, about fifty small dark men in a half-circle in the evening shadows.

Something rustled down the rock from above, and the Mimi dropped beside him and seized her loop of cord.

'It's all right,' he muttered at her. 'They've felt the power.' He looked at them sternly again and they stared sternly back. He knew he must try to speak to them.

'You hear me?' he asked.

Some of them nodded. One grunted words that sounded like 'Got ears.' The rest went on staring from under their brows.

'The land sent me,' said Wirrun.

They grunted quietly together and again one of them spoke to him: 'No fire.'

The words went all around the half-circle. 'No fire,' they grunted sternly. 'No fire.' 'No fire.'

'You've put it out,' said Wirrun, 'but you might need it yet. The ice is coming.'

They grunted to each other and to him in an angry chorus. 'No ice.' 'Gone very long.' 'Done for last time.' 'No ice.'

'The land knows,' said Wirrun, 'and the earth-people know. And you know. The ice is coming back. The ice people, the Ninya, are close by now coming inside the rocks. I don't know where they are but they're not far.

This,' he showed them the power, 'and this,' he patted
the rock, 'say you must help me fight the ice.'

They looked from him to the Mimi and at each
other. 'No fire,' they grunted. 'No fire.'

'Never mind that,' said Wirrun sternly. 'Who are
you, any rate?'

They replied with a chorus of grunts too many and
fast for him to follow. He turned to the Mimi as an
interpreter.

'They are the Wa-tha-gun-darl,' she said. 'They live
only here, in caves and among these rocks. They do not
go inside the rock like rock-spirits, but I think they
have felt the ice far off with no real knowing. They say
they will have no fire lest it bring strangers; they hunt
birds and eat them raw. The big ants, the fierce biters,
the bulldog ants, are theirs. If a stranger angers them
they place him on the nests of the bulldog ants and hold
him there till he dies.'

'Do they, now?' said Wirrun sourly. He could still
feel those little iron arms dragging him from the rock.
He did not think he would have had much chance against
the Wa-tha-gun-darl and the bulldog ants. The half-
circle faced him silently, half seen in the soft light between evening and young moonlight. 'Little toughs,'
muttered Wirrun, and spoke to them again.

'You'd better hear this and remember,' he said. 'The
Ninya will be going through in the rocks somewhere
near, some time soon, on their way south. They're looking for the Eldest Nargun, the one that makes fire and
fought them before. If they find it and freeze it they'll
come out of the rocks and build the ice again. Here,
everywhere, all over the land. They'll freeze the lot of
you, and your bulldog ants too. So you'd better help
me find the Eldest Nargun first. Now then: tell me. Do
you know this Eldest Nargun?'

They looked at each other and grunted softly, then
began to speak out. 'Know that Nargun long time gone.'
'Very long time not see that Nargun.' 'Don't know now.
Not see that Nargun.' There was a background of fur-

ther grunting that Wirrun could not follow, and he turned
to the Mimi again.

'They keep to themselves in their own country,' she
told him. 'They see no one, save sometimes the Nyols
who are small like themselves and live within the rocks.
It is not a thing they would know, for their knowing is
small.'

'All right,' said Wirrun, glad to have it over. 'But if
you see any of these Nyols you'd better ask them. Keep
your eyes and ears open, and if you find out anything
about the Ninya or the Nargun you'd better send me a
message somehow. If you can.' They grunted together
and nodded, but he thought they were not likely to
help. They had no way of sending any message that he
could understand, and they themselves never left their
hill. At least he had warned them of the Ninya.

'Right,' he said. 'Now, we've been travelling all day
and we're off again before morning.' Weariness flooded
over him as soon as he let the thought of it enter his
mind. 'So we're going to eat here, see?'

'No fire,' they grunted at once. He ignored that.

'And after that we're going to sleep till the moon
sets. And I don't want any tomfooling while we're
asleep, see? No tricks, no ants, hands off.'

In the moonlight the little men were only a dark half-
circle of gleaming eyes, but he heard their angry buzz-
ing. 'What's up now?' he asked the Mimi. 'Don't they
even want us to sleep on their precious hill?'

'You have angered them,' she said severely. 'They
are angry that you think they will hurt us as we sleep.
They say that if they wished to hurt us they would do it
now or it would already be done. They say they have
no need to creep on sleeping strangers and that they too
belong to the land.'

'Let's hope they remember, then,' said Wirrun unre-
pentantly, for death by bulldog ants is a very unpleas-
ant death and his struggle with the little men had left a
strong impression on his mind. He stood up and walked
firmly to his pack. The Wa-tha-gun-darl had not begun

to deal with it at the time they discovered the power, and it lay untouched where he had left it. They squatted where they were and continued to watch while he unrolled his sleeping-bag and prepared to eat his meatballs cold from the can. 'You ought to eat something,' he said to the Mimi. 'Why don't you try a bit of this?'

She had trusted the Wa-tha-gun-darl enough to let go the cord to the power. She sniffed at the meatballs, catsneezed, and shook her head. Wirrun was too weary to think any further and could only draw a little water for her from his canvas bag. 'Have to get that filled tomorrow,' he said, feeling its lightness.

There was a stir in the watching half-circle, and a figure moving to and fro. Then one of the little people moved forward, laid something on the rock with gruntings, and moved back. The Mimi picked up the object and bent her head to the watchers. She showed Wirrun what she held: a small green parrot, dead and limp.

He wrinkled his nose at it. 'Can you eat that raw?'

'It is good food and all they can give,' she said. 'I have eaten raw meat for many days now.' She began to tear out the feathers and eat.

When Wirrun had finished his meal he offered the empty tin to the dark watchers, pushing it down the rock towards their crouching shapes. 'Your ants'd like to clean that up,' he told them.

One of them picked it up cautiously, sniffed at it, and passed it quickly to the next. They passed it from hand to hand all along the half-circle, sniffing at it and grunting with dislike. Then one of them took it away down the hill. While they were doing this the Mimi slipped away into the rock. Wirrun stowed his gear safely beside him, hung the water-bag back on its branch, and got into his sleeping-bag. Though he was so tired he knew it would be hard to sleep with the fierce little people watching and grunting.

While he was thinking this he heard a stirring like leaves, and when he looked the dark half-circle of watchers had melted. The hill seemed empty against the stars; but just before he dropped into sleep it seemed to him that in the moonlight someone was still watching. . . .

He was wakened in darkness by a small strong hand pulling at him. He sat up quickly. The moon had gone; the stars and the sharp coolness of night told him that it was now about two in the morning. Three of the strong little men stood by him.

'Sleep too much,' one of them grunted. 'Moon gone, you go.'

Wirrun yawned. 'Thanks,' he said to the Wa-tha-gundarl; but he thought they were more anxious to see him gone from their hill than concerned about his journey.

The small men nodded and moved away to the edge of the rock, and the Mimi stood beside Wirrun as he fastened his pack. 'Have a good rest?' he asked; and then he saw that she was quivering.

'I have not rested,' she said softly. 'I have lain outside the rock lest these people think I did not trust them. The cold wind is blowing.'

Wirrun woke up sharply. 'What—in there? Did you feel it?'

She shook her head. 'I was in the rock. It was colder than rock. Deeper in there are caverns. I heard the wind howling.'

Wirrun wrenched at the straps on his pack. At last he knew where the Ninya were. They were here.

'Time we got going,' he said urgently. 'After all that time on the wind I thought we'd be a bit ahead.' He saw that she carried a bundle of leaves tied firmly with grass cord. 'Here: do you want to put that in one of these pockets? You don't want to carry it.'

She hesitated, gave it to him, and watched him fasten it into a pocket. He lifted down his water-bag and hefted it, frowning in surprise. Its weight told him that it had been filled. The three little men were watching closely and silently. He turned to them and gave them a small bow.

'Thanks,' he said. 'Very good water.' He bowed again.

They nodded and seemed pleased.

In silence, in the dimness of starlight with the Mimi holding her cord again, they set off down the hill. The three small men came after them, and shadowy out of the darkness came more until a little crowd followed them down the hill. At the foot of the hill they stopped, still watching. Seeing this Wirrun paused and spoke to them.

'Thanks for having us,' he said; and however odd it sounded he wasn't joking. 'The cold wind's blowing now, right inside those rocks up there, so watch out for the Ninya. If you need any help send word.'

They nodded and grunted. 'We send,' they said; and, 'Good journey.'

Wirrun turned and went on with a lighter heart, for now he knew the little Wa-tha-gun-darl had done their best to help. They had given the Mimi that bird last night, and whatever it was that she carried when he woke. They had filled his water-bag, watched while he slept, wakened him at the proper time, brought him safely to the edge of their country, and wished him good journey. Fierce they might be, and tough, but they could have done no more than this. They had spoken truly: they too belonged to the land.

He and the Mimi walked on and found the highway, a hard black line in the dark. 'We'll stick to this for a bit,' said Wirrun, 'till we know where we are. It's near the coast, any rate.' The Mimi said nothing; perhaps she knew exactly where they were in earth-spirit terms that Wirrun could not grasp.

Very soon the highway went over a bridge, and black letters on a white board could be read by starlight when Wirrun peered close enough. 'Tilba-Tilba,' he said, calling the map into mind, and he frowned anxiously. 'Just as well we had that wind, I reckon it took us a hundred and twenty or thirty miles. With that and the train we've come a long way, a lot faster than I thought we could. And still we find the Ninya nearly here.' He shook his head. 'They're going fast.'

'The spirits will not help them,' said the Mimi.

'M'm. They haven't helped us much yet. Still and all,

we haven't had the chance to meet many. And maybe we're still a bit far from the right country. The ones that live in the Narguns' country ought to know more.'

He quickened his pace, striding down the highway at his best speed, and the Mimi loped easily beside him keeping up without trouble. It made him remember how she had overtaken him after the train journey, and he thought she might well have raced the Ninya without him to hold her back.

'Ko-in should've given you the power instead of me,' he growled.

She gave her sneezing snort. 'Stiffen your spine, Man. You do well enough when you do not hurl me from the sky like a spear. The Ninya are near but they have not found the Eldest of Narguns.'

'All right, all right, quit nagging,' said Wirrun, but he felt a little better.

'A man looks forward too far and backward not enough,' said the Mimi. 'But the earth needs him. I could not come alone. The spirit knew what he did when he gave you the power.'

In the black wall of trees on their left a cavern appeared and Wirrun looked for the road that turned into it off the highway. It was a gravel road, narrow and dark between trees, and its surface soon became rutted and rough. But Wirrun laid his hand on the power and felt the silent strength of it, and the land around and beneath. He walked surely on the rough track and was glad to be away from the highway. In half an hour they came out of the trees within sound of the sea. The stars lit them again; and in a little while they saw the darkly glinting restless field of the sea with pale stretches of beach and dark shapes of headlands, and it seemed almost as light as moonlight.

For some time the track ran between the sea and a wide sand-locked lagoon. The night was growing pale when they passed it and walked between sea and land: a half-dark movement and a hushed, forever, crying on the left where the stars swept down, and a watching stillness shadowed with hill and forest on the right.

Light and dark, cold and thaw, age on age, all is mine, said the sea.

I am. I will be. I rise out of time, said the land.

Wirrun and the Mimi walked between them by track and causeway and bridge: past a sleeping township while the stars went out and a small wind stirred, across inlets and on while the sun came out of the sea. And in the early sunlight by another sand-locked lake they sat down to rest and eat. Wirrun gave the Mimi her leaf-wrapped package out of which she took a dead wren.

'Do you want that?' asked Wirrun. 'There might be oysters. Or you could try a bit of bread and cheese.'

'The bird is good,' said the Mimi shortly, tearing out feathers. She slipped the loop of cord over her wrist and turned a questing face to the breeze. 'The right wind comes again,' she told him.

'It does?' said Wirrun, cutting a hunk of cheese. 'Maybe that's luck. Only I'm not sure we should take it.'

'You cry for speed because the Ninya are near, and the land hears. The land calls up the wind.'

'You reckon? But we gotta choose. If we ride the wind we don't meet any spirits, and we can't ask our way to this Eldest Nargun.'

The Mimi hissed. 'You think too much and know too little.'

'You said I couldn't help it,' Wirrun retorted; but he lay back on the land with his mouth full of cheese and the sun warming him, and let the sound of the sea pass over. When they had finished, and had drunk some of the water the Wa-tha-gun-darl had given them, he said, 'Come on then, is this wind ready yet?'

'Soon,' said the Mimi; and they walked on a little across the mouth of the lake with the wind coming stronger at their shoulders. When they had walked about a mile she said, 'Turn with me now and run,' and Wirrun closed his hand on the power and ran with her.

They were caught up into the wind and tumbled higher, and rode again above the broken coast; and the sea dreamed again below and Wirrun dreamed that he flew with gulls. But the gulls dropped away and slipped off in a current of wind, and other broader wings beat about Wirrun and the Mimi. There were a dozen great birds shining in the morning sun, birds that Wirrun had never seen before, like hawks but bigger. One of them called to him shrill and sharp across the wind.

'What man rides the wind with a rock-spirit at his side and magic at his belt?'

Then Wirrun saw that these were spirits too, but he was already clutching the power.

Two

The great white bird-spirits swung on their broad wings under, over, and around Wirrun and the Mimi. Now and then one of them diverted the wind so that the two wind-riders went spinning or slipping for a moment. Nervously the Mimi twisted her legs together and pulled on her loop of cord to draw herself closer to Wirrun. He himself was not afraid, for who can watch the flight of birds without delight? He shouted back boldly to the spirit that had called to him.

'I'm Wirrun of the People! Who are you?'

'Yauruks!' screamed the spirit, and the others screamed too so that they sounded as well as looked like a flock of great sea-birds.

'Yauruks! Yauruks! We are Yauruks!'

'Do you come from the sea?' shouted Wirrun.

The bird-spirits swung overhead so that he could see their soft under-feathers ruffled by the wind.

'Land!' they shrieked.

'We come from land!'

'We hunt whales for the People!'

'Whales?' Wirrun was astonished. He turned his head to the Mimi. 'What do the People want with whales?'

'A man should know that,' she cried in his ear. 'A whale is meat for a tribe.'

'Whales!' the Yauruks were screeching. 'We hunt them to land!' 'We drive them ashore!' 'Whales for the People!' They were the loveliest, liveliest, happiest spirits that Wirrun had yet seen, and even when their great wings beat too near they charmed him.

'Why does a man ride the wind?' one of them shrieked, and he remembered his journey and his quest. It was hard to shout an answer through the wind while the great wings beat close and swung off again, but he did his best.

'The ice is coming again!' he shouted. 'The Ninya are hunting the Eldest Nargun, and if they trap it the ice will come! I'm looking for the Nargun, to warn it!'

'The ice!' they shrieked. 'The ice! The ice!' They drew away on each side and flew in silence at a little distance. Wirrun waited for them to come close again so that he could shout his question; but soon they spiralled up and flew at a great height into the sun and away to sea. Wirrun watched them out of sight, hunching his shoulders in disappointment.

'You did not ask if they knew the Eldest of Narguns,' the Mimi hissed in his ear.

'I know. I was trying. Any rate I told 'em. If they'd known they would've said.'

She turned her round dark eyes on him in silence.

They rode high on the wind for about three hours and saw high rugged mountains ahead, reaching across the land towards the sea; and stony-backed hills facing the dreaming sea; and tall headlands of rock standing over it and broad shelves of rock reaching into it; and Wirrun grew restless and uneasy. Where hill and rock stood so near the sea the Ninya might be too, for they were travelling fast. And soon the coast would begin its sharp turn west, and still he knew nothing of the Eldest Nargun.

'We'll go down,' he said to the Mimi. 'We'll find a place to sleep for the day, and tonight we'll walk all night and not just a few hours.'

At once she began to twist herself into a tight protective knot. Wirrun sighed.

'All right,' he said, 'I know. I'm supposed to loosen my fingers a bit and tighten up again, and keep on doing it all the way down. Right?'

She untwisted again. And when Wirrun tried it he found that this method worked well. If he loosened his hold on the power too much at one time it was like coming down a bumpy staircase of wind and the Mimi glared at him, but when he had it right he could bring them down at a steep or a gradual slant.

They crossed a wide bay with towns around its shores and a busy population of Happy Folk. When these were past Wirrun came sloping down into forested hills with only a lighthouse in sight. He used the staircase method to drop them between trees on a hillside. The Mimi landed twisted up and Wirrun with a stumble and a fall, but it was much better than his last landing. There was only the stone-heavy feeling again, and the sense of the land still blowing past, but even these passed off quickly.

Wirrun rubbed his aching fingers. 'Too soon to eat again,' he said, for it was not yet noon. 'We'll sleep till evening, and I'll light a fire for a proper meal before we start again.'

'Fires, eating, and sleep,' gibed the Mimi. 'It is slow work being a man.'

Wirrun was nettled, for they might have ridden the wind all day and travelled far. Only his anxiety had brought them down, his need to be near the hills with the land under his feet so that he could watch and listen; and he was not at all sure that he had been right. 'I reckon,' he said shortly, 'that by wind and walking we've done around a couple of hundred miles in two days, and I can't help being a man. Do you want to keep going?'

She drooped and shook her head. 'You are the thinker and the pace is yours,' she said; and he was sorry, for he saw that she had been teasing again.

'Will you try the rocks?' he said. 'I'll wait and see if you're all right. There's no wind here in the trees.'

Above in the treetops the wind was mimicking the sea, but in the forest there was warm and summery stillness. The Mimi dropped her cord. It took more courage to try the rocks now that they knew the Ninya were near, but rocks loomed all along the hillside. She went to the nearest, blew on it, and slipped into its gaping dark. Wirrun waited for a while, making a sleeping place for himself under that rock while he waited. In ten minutes she had not come out, so he lay on his sleeping-bag in the heavy warmth of the day and let his mind slip free.

It went backwards, past the teasing Mimi and the Yauruks crying over the sea in search of whales, back to the angry little Wa-tha-gun-darl dragging him to their ants; and then to the cold wind howling in their hill. He thought of the old south land lying burdened again under ice and snow; the great red rocks in its tired old heart cracked and tilted again; its far tender hazes washed into white; its fragile grey shrubs and slender lines of forest beaten in their long fight for life. And for comfort he put his hand on its stony clay.

Sleep now, and dream no dreams, said the land.

So Wirrun thought of Ko-in and the mountain; and in an hour he slept.

He woke with the forest shadowed in evening and coolness flowing up from the sea. The Mimi was beside him, having wakened him with leaves. She laid her twigs of fingers on his face to quieten him and they felt like a spider. She pointed through shadows to the hillside behind. Wirrun rolled over without speaking and looked.

At first he saw nothing but shadows, and then a movement of shadows. As he kept looking there were little shadowy shapes slipping out of the rocks and away among the trees. He put his hand on the power and saw that they were little grey spirits about as big as the ant-people, but these were more spidery in shape and not so fierce and angry. The power throbbed in his hand and he unfastened it from his belt and began to unwind the cord. After a moment of thought he held out the power to the Mimi while he himself held the loop of the cord.

She hesitated with her dark eyes on his face, then took the soft-hard thing in her hands with awe. Her tall thin shape, as silent and shadowy as the others but blending more quickly with trees and grass, slithered away and vanished. Wirrun held his end of the cord and waited for her to lay a trail of it along the hillside and back. He could not see her at all—but he saw two spirits from the rocks suddenly halt in their flight down the hill and turn this way and that. Then the Mimi was beside him again, having waited till the two spirits were in her trap before she closed it behind them.

The two trapped spirits darted here and there along the line of cord looking for a way past, and so came at last to where Wirrun and the Mimi were silently waiting. They would have flickered off again, but the Mimi held up the power and Wirrun said, 'Stop.' Then they stood there, two little grey people with eyes that flashed like tiny stars.

They did not seem at all nervous but looked Wirrun up and down, yet he saw them glance at the power with reluctant respect. 'You wrestle?' one of them invited in a voice that rumbled like stones.

Wirrun was not tempted to accept this offer. The Watha-gun-darl had taught him to respect the powers of little people, and he did not think these two would have offered to wrestle if they had not been sure of winning. He thought he knew what had made them flee in such numbers from their rocks inside the hill, and he came to the point at once.

'The land sent me,' he said, 'and you know this power. You're running off because the cold wind's blowing in the rocks and the ice is coming.'

They looked at him with their star-like eyes and said nothing.

'What people are you?' Wirrun asked.

'We Nyols,' they said. Wirrun thought he had heard that name before and looked at the Mimi.

'They are rock-spirits,' she told him. 'They are the people known to the Wa-tha-gun-darl.' She added, 'I have been in the rocks. The cold wind is not yet blowing.'

'Not blowing?' Wirrun looked at the two Nyols. 'Why are you running off, then?'

'Not yet blowing,' said one, and the other added, 'Soon.'

'Right. Now listen.' Two pairs of bright eyes were at once fixed on him, yet he felt they measured him like wrestlers and not in any awe. They would listen, and then they would do as they wished. He spoke distinctly. 'The Ninya make the cold wind: the people of the ice. They go through here to hunt the Eldest Nargun. You know it?'

They nodded. 'We know Narguns.'

For a moment Wirrun's heart leapt. It was the first time any creature had admitted knowing anything. 'But the Eldest,' he said. 'The one that calls up fire. You know that one?'

They looked at each other, conversing in their rumbling voices with nods and head-shakes. 'Very big Nargun, that one.' 'Very clever, very old.' 'Not see that Nargun now.' 'Not see for a very long time.'

'If the Ninya find that Nargun first,' said Wirrun still with care, 'they'll freeze it and build the ice again. You don't want that, do you?'

They thought about it. 'Build ice on land,' they said. 'Better than in rocks.' They nodded wisely.

'But,' argued Wirrun, 'if *I* find that Nargun first, the Ninya will go home to their own country and build no ice at all. That's better still, isn't it?' They thought again and nodded. 'Now tell me: where is the Eldest Nargun?'

They conversed with each other again. 'That very old Nargun, that first one with the fire,' they told one another. 'Not see that Nargun a very long time,' they re-

minded each other. 'Gone, that First One. Gone from
our country.' They turned to Wirrun, having worked it
out between them. 'Gone into the sea,' they said.

'Into the sea? Are you sure?' They nodded. 'Whereabouts, then?' They looked at him with their twinkling
eyes and said nothing.

The Mimi said softly, 'They do not know where.'

'In the sea of its country,' said one of the Nyols.
'You wrestle?' it invited again.

'No, I won't wrestle, I got no time,' said Wirrun,
nodding to the Mimi who slipped off to rewind the
cord. 'And if I did I'd win because I've got a very great
magic. Now look, if you want to dodge the ice you tell
your people to go north to the people with the bulldog
ants. You know those people. The cold wind was blowing up there last night, so it ought to be past by now—
finish—coming this way. You can get behind it if you
go north.' He nodded to the Nyols, and like shadows
they flitted away down the hill.

The Mimi had rewound the power in its possum-fur
cord and stood holding it out to him on her two hands.
He took it, thanked her, and sat staring at it cupped in
his own hands. The Mimi watched him; she could see
that he was thinking. She crept off and made a fire in
the shelter of a deep angle of rock. Its yellow light
broke into Wirrun's thinking, and he got up and went to
the fire. He noticed that at some time during the day
the Mimi had supplied herself with a root and a lizard.

'Thanks for waking me,' he said, rummaging in his
supplies and finding mostly potatoes. 'In the sea, they
said. Do you reckon they really know?'

'They know what they have heard,' said the Mimi. 'It
is one fibre of knowing. There will be other spirits.'

'They don't seem all that anxious to help,' said Wirrun. 'Ko-in reckoned they would when they saw the
power.'

'He said they must help, for it is a great power
known in all countries. He did not say that because of it
they would *wish* to help.' He stared at her under his
brows. 'Man,' she cried suddenly, 'you know nothing!

They are small creatures of the earth, in doubt and fear of the ice! Do the ants wish to help you when their nest is broken? Do the shadows and the streams turn aside to help you? The spirits will help if they must, and if they can they will hide. Have you forgotten why *I* help?'

He looked at her in distress, and she drooped a little under his gaze. 'You!' he cried. She just stood there holding her lightly roasted lizard by the tail. But then Wirrun laughed and shook his head. 'No, not you,' he said. 'You help a lot more than you must. You're an ice-fighter, you poor frail hider, you.'

'I help,' said the Mimi sadly, 'because then you must send me home.' Wirrun laughed again, shaking his head. 'And because the land sends you.' He laughed again.

'And because you remember the ice,' he told her. 'These little things, I reckon they'd rather forget. Maybe some of 'em never knew.' He broke open a roasted potato and loaded it with butter, but she could see that he was thinking again.

'In the sea . . .' he murmured. 'Once the Ninya know that, they can stop looking. Fire's not much good in the sea.'

She cat-sneezed at him. 'And what is to keep the Eldest in the sea? Since it chose to go there, the Ninya will know it may choose to come out.'

'What's to keep it in the sea? Ice. Ice will keep it there.'

'Must a Mimi give courage to a man?' she hissed. 'You will call it out of the sea!'

'And that's more than I bargained for. A creature of rock . . . and the sea's full of rocks round here. Someone's got to know this Eldest Nargun. Someone's got to show me the very rock—with the Ninya right on my tail all the way.'

'While you sit and eat by the fire like a man, and the night passes.'

She had eaten and drunk quickly, and to her Wirrun's meals were always enormous. But he finished this one, complaining that she was nagging again, and buried the fire and rolled his pack.

The fall of a gully led them down through a darkness of trees. They came out of the forest on a moonlit shore and found a track. The tide had turned and the sea cried savagely, tossing a black and silver net of a beauty so dangerous that Wirrun was almost afraid to look at it. All down the long coast the same sea cried and tossed its dark-bright net; and away to the south it caught the Eldest Nargun.

Around it on the shelf of rock, broken rocks shouldered aside the tossing sea. The Nargun crouched among them and knew itself greater than they. For it was old, a First Thing; it ached and was weary with age. And though it lay in the cold bright sea, yet it had the power of fire.

It was days since the Nargun had crushed and eaten the fish, and sea-things have memories as short as things on land. They had come back to creep under it and shelter from the crashing tide. A crab pressed close to the rock under its edge. At its feet a tangle of weed wrapped close, fanned out, wrapped in again; and folded under this curtain hung the fish. An anemone clung tight closed in a crevice. Triton, whelk, and limpet had locked themselves to the Nargun's sides.

The monster's blind and ancient love was for man moving warm in the sun. There was no love here; but there was the hidden secret of life. The Nargun nurtured this. It spread its weight on the rock beneath. When the tide tugged it cried aloud to the moon, and its cry was as far and as cold as the moon's silver.

And while it cried and fought the sea Wirrun and the Mimi sought it, striding between the sea and the brooding land; and behind them in the forests the Nyols fled north; and on the hill of the Wa-tha-gun-darl a battle was raging.

Three

The fierce little people of the hill had done their evening's hunting at the time when the birds were nesting for the night. Now they were crouching and sitting and lying together in one big cave, pulling the feathers from their dead birds and tearing the raw flesh with their teeth. As they ate they grunted quietly together, about the evening's hunt or in satisfaction at the one meal of their day.

They grunted too about the strangers who had come out of the sky to visit them last night, for this was a big event and the strangers were the first they had seen for many years. Though they had been bound to help these two they did not welcome strangers. Once or twice a year they enjoyed a corroboree with the Nyols, whom they had known for an age or so and who were friends; but even these friends they did not welcome too often. The Wa-tha-gun-darl were a tribe who kept to themselves, as fierce in their affection for each other as they were in defending themselves from outsiders. Men they had always distrusted, and other spirits they kept at arm's length. By day they hid, and by night they would have no fire or light to bring strangers to their hill.

So now they crouched in their tribal cave, grunting companionably together and building up little heaps of feathers between them as they ate. The dimness of the cave hid the brightness of the feathers: rust of swallow, blue of wren, bronze of thrush, yellow of thornbill, green of lorikeet, all faded into grey. Outside the dusk was beginning to blend into moonlight. The Wa-tha-gun-darl watched it in content; later the moonlight would tempt them into games, and perhaps to dance.

A cold breath moved in the cave, and the heaps of feathers stirred. The little men fell silent, turning dark eyes to each other and behind them into the cave. Wind may curl out of a cave when it has first blown in, but outside the evening was still.

The feathers fluttered like injured birds. The breath became a breeze, knife-edged with cold. Silently the small dark men dropped their food and grasped the heavy sticks that lay about them on the rock. Silently they melted out of the cave and vanished.

The sky grew softly bright with the moon and was hung with stars. The cold that gushed from the cave was bitter; the wind carried feathers like the flying ghosts of birds. In their hiding places the little men shivered and grasped their sticks more tightly. They waited.

The dark cave-mouth caught a sparkle from the moon, as if it were quartz instead of granite. Out of it stepped a man, all white, who sparkled too in the moonlight. He stood there, tall as a man and white as a cloud, but sparkling. He looked towards the sea and along the hill; and then he turned to look at the dark forest above.

Small black shapes darted from hiding, sticks swung and smashed. The white man toppled and the sticks beat at him. Broken ice flew in the moonlight. The man lay smashed; white blood came out of him and spread on the ground.

The little dark men slipped back into their places. From nooks and shadows of rock they watched the broken man and saw the ground where he lay whitening and sparkling with frost, and long icicles growing from the mouth of their tribal cave. The wind blew on.

The frost grew. In the ground, hidden spear-heads of ice were forming. Across the mouth of the cave something gleamed and glittered in the moonlight: ice was building there. There were creaks and whispers; the little men watched and listened. Soon they saw that a wall of ice was building fast across the mouth of their cave. Angrily they rushed into the moonlight, grunting fiercely and brandishing their sticks. Frost bit them and spears of ice cut their feet as they ran; that made them angrier. Slipping on frost and struggling up again they beat at the wall of ice.

Ice-crystals flew and sparkled. The centre of the ice wall creaked and cracked—they flew at it with their sticks, but it strengthened even while they smashed. And the wall grew higher. In places it was clear and deep like water; through there they could see white shapes that moved and laughed.

Some of the beating sticks were broken, and small men rushed to find new weapons. Their shouts made the others swing round: a second wall of ice was building behind them, its ends curving in to meet the first. They saw that the ice was walling them in, and they threw themselves at the outer wall.

It was already almost two feet high. When they tried to climb their hands and feet stuck to the ice; they had to pull themselves or each other free. And while they struggled the walls grew, both in height and in thickness.

One of them seized a broken stick and pressed it against the ice until it froze there. Quickly more broken weapons were found and frozen into place to make a ladder. The Wa-tha-gun-darl began swarming up the wall even while those at the rear were building a second ladder.

Green eyes in sparkling frost-white faces were looking over the wall from the cave. The Ninya watched the Wa-tha-gun-darl escaping. Now they could let the ice melt, and sticks and small men slide down, or they could build the wall faster. They built faster.

The Wa-tha-gun-darl climbed and leapt, froze to the wall and tore themselves free, clamped on more sticks as the first were frozen over and buried in ice. The two walls built towards each other. The space between them grew narrower; dropped and broken weapons disappeared under them; there was no more material for building ladders. The last four little dark men could not climb.

Those on the outside screamed and grunted in fury. They laid branches against the outer wall to climb up, tried to lower branches into the narrowing space inside, clamped sticks and stones to the inside and grunted, 'Leap! Leap!' But the captive four were weaker, dazed with cold and the pain of torn skin. They could only run a little up and down the narrow space. And the walls grew and joined, shining under the moon.

Looking through clear ice, the Wa-tha-gun-darl could see a dark blur here and there. They beat at the wall with stones and sticks, froze to it and tore free, cut their feet on hidden spears of ice. There was now a single block of ice ten feet long, five feet high, and seven feet thick. From behind it came a cold crackle of laughter, fading as the Ninya went back into the cave.

The little men fought on while the moon went down, sending powdered crystals flying and sometimes breaking off large chunks. But the great block of ice stood solid, though its surface was beginning to melt and trickle. One by one the fighters fell back, dazed and exhausted. They lay or squatted in despair, shivering and bleeding, staring with hopeless eyes at the ice.

That was how the Nyols found them.

The Nyols fleeing from the coming cold had met it flowing in a tide down the Wa-tha-gun-darl's hill. They had stood for a while, chattering, shivering, pointing. What drew them on was their knowledge of the Wa-tha-gun-darl, the fierce little fighters who lived only on this hill, who would not have been driven off and had no place to flee. Huddled together in a body, watching bright-eyed in the starlight, the Nyols advanced up the hill.

When they saw the hopeless, exhausted shapes and the great gleaming ice they wanted to run. They also wanted to help their friends, and most of all to know what had happened. Their first move chanced to be forward, and after that they forgot about running.

They dragged the Wa-tha-gun-darl into caves,

dressed their wounds with leaves, heaped earth over them for warmth, and gave them water and the blood of lizards. They rumbled to each other softly, exchanging news and putting together the grunted words they gathered from one or another of the wounded; and at last, gathering their courage and their curiosity, they ventured by ways of their own into the rocks.

From there they found a way under the ice and, digging and hacking upward, dragged out four small still bodies. These they laid within the rock and stood around them at a loss, not speaking or looking at each other. They had not before known any death among their kind. After a time they went back to their patients, leaving little bodies in the rock, and told those who could listen what they had found and done.

In one of the caves a Wa-tha-gun-darl man stirred and grunted weakly. A Nyol bent to listen.

'Message. Man with magic.'

The Nyol nodded and slipped away.

And inside the hills, deep in caverns where the wind howled, the Ninya rested and laughed. To them it had not been a battle but only a small skirmish, yet they were excited. They had won the skirmish, and they had built their first good ice in the moonlight. Their beards bristled and gleamed in the twilight as they laughed together. Only their leader paced the cavern and frowned. In time their green eyes turned to him and their laughter crackled into silence. He saw them looking.

'We are one short,' he growled angrily.

They creaked with laughter. 'Even one short we built fast. We gave him a grave of beauty. And how it shone! Brighter than the stars!'

He crackled with anger. 'Oh yes, we built fast: there was no fire in our faces. But one of us was smashed by a thing no bigger than a stone.' He glared at them. 'He should have no grave of beauty, for he betrayed us. A man who walks upright from a cave into a stick betrays us all. If you would take the land and build the ice, then watch the man beside you. Let him not betray you with his death, for you need him. We come near the country of the Eldest of Narguns.'

They looked sideways at each other; yet they could not help their grins and hid them in sparkling beards or frosty fingers. Their leader paced among them full of anger and rounded on them again.

'Those small things that were captive, why did you give them to the ice? Why did you not bring them alive to me?'

They only looked at him under their icicle brows, not understanding. He howled at them.

'Where then is the Nargun, the Eldest? How shall we find it in its country? Tell me that!'

They did not tell him for they did not know.

'But the spirits know!' he roared at them. 'The spirits of these countries, they can tell us! And you give them to the ice and waste our journey!'

'They know,' growled a voice, 'but that is not to tell. They will tell us nothing.'

'Not for love, or the ice,' the leader growled back. 'But for fear they might, or for life itself. If you would not live for ever in a cave then bring me a spirit of this country and I will make it tell.'

They crowded together and growled softly to each other. From the crowd one voice creaked out again.

'The mighty leader of the Ninya has said that the Eldest will come of itself: that it will come from anywhere within knowing and stand in our path and redden the rocks with fire. Has the great and mighty leader not spoken truly?'

There were icy titters. The leader glared.

'Was I not right? Have I not led you safely though we searched no caverns?'

'Oh, you were right, great leader. We believe you even now. Therefore we need not search through the country of the Narguns. If we find a quiet place by the coast and away from men, if we build a great ice and wait and watch beside it, then the Eldest will come to us.'

The leader frowned in thought for a moment. He lifted his head. 'Truly a wonder, a marvel beyond

snow: a man who thinks as one of the Ninya and not as
a child of the People. This we will do.'

They howled with joy and stamped till the frost flew,
and when they were quiet he spoke again.

'Yet still you will bring me a spirit if you can take
one. For the caves smother you, and you wait and
watch badly, and we will lose no knowing that we can
find. Now let us go forward again as fast as the caverns
will take us.'

So the Ninya went on fast in the path of the wind.
The caverns twisted back and forth, and plunged down
crevices and broke into cliffs and narrowed into clefts;
they were threaded with streams and floored with lakes
and grew heavy with ice; but always their windings
turned south again at last, as Wirrun and the Mimi
walked south by the shore.

The young man of the People and the rock-spirit of
the north walked far that night. While the moon lasted
their walking was quick and easy, and when it was gone
the sea reflected the starlight and Wirrun kept a hand
on the power. It was as well he did, for they might have
been attacked by an earth-spirit.

They had just rested for a short time and eaten and
drunk. The track had turned some way inland; they
were walking between heath and banksia on the left and
under a forested hill on the right. They were silent, as
they mostly were. There was only the mourning of the
sea. Suddenly three loud cracks rang through the silence.

Wirrun turned a startled face to the Mimi. 'It is some
spirit,' she said.

They stood still and searched the darkness all around
them; but the Dulugar came from above, flying down
from the hill. If they had known it he was a sign that
the spirits were restless and uneasy; for the Dulugar's
place was in the higher hills farther back and its usual
habit was to attack women of the People.

It came hurtling down in their path and made a lunge
at them—but Wirrun held the power and the Mimi its
cord. The Dulugar hesitated and its arms fell. It was a

great strong shape like a man with long arms and short legs, and covered with hair like a dog. It peered first at Wirrun and then at the Mimi—peered more closely—and broke into loud rude laughter. The Mimi's tall stick-figure, big-eared and possum-eyed, was not the female shape that the Dulugar was used to.

The Mimi bristled with fury. 'Ask it quickly and order it off,' she hissed.

Wirrun was angry too, for the laughter was coarse and rude and the Dulugar's sudden appearance had startled him. He took a step forward with the power, and the great black shape stopped laughing and stepped back.

'Whatever you are,' said Wirrun, 'you can stop right there and speak. The land sent us because the ice is coming.' The Dulugar looked from side to side in a hunted way. It would have shuffled off, but Wirrun had ordered it to stay.

'None of that,' he warned again. 'Here's one with me not a tenth your size but she rode the winds right across the land to fight the ice. If a great big lump like you can't fight, any rate you can talk. Say where the Eldest Nargun is, the one that calls up fire.'

The hairy thing snorted like a horse. 'That old rock,' it said in a thick voice. 'No one sees that rock now. Went into the sea, that rock did.'

The sea again? Wirrun frowned. 'Whereabouts?' he asked. 'Is it far from here?'

'Off this coast. Off its own country,' the Dulugar said. 'Not far.'

'Off here?' said Wirrun keenly. 'Off this country? Is this the country of the Narguns?'

The Dulugar snorted. 'Country of the Dulugar,' it said. 'Narguns live here too,' it added.

Wirrun would have needed a map and daylight to know exactly where they were, but he knew they had probably crossed the Victorian border during the night and were near the place where the coast turned west. If this creature lived in the Narguns' own country it must surely know where the Eldest could be found.

'I want to know which spot,' he said. 'The ice people are after it, and I gotta find it first.'

But the Dulugar shook its head. 'Don't go in the sea,' it said. 'Don't know where that old rock is.'

Wirrun was bitterly disappointed and glared at it for some time, but the Dulugar could only tell what it knew. 'All right,' he growled at last. 'Clear off and behave yourself. And if you see the ice people, the Ninya, see if you can't help instead of hiding like a great loon.'

The Dulugar snorted again and sidled off into the dark. When it had gone a little way it broke into the same rude laughter, and so flew off still laughing to the hills.

'Come,' said the Mimi stiffly. She had to tug at the cord, for Wirrun was thinking again. He broke into his long stride beside her murmuring, 'The sea. . . .'

'You cannot change what is known,' said the Mimi. 'You can only know it, and maybe before the Ninya know it.'

That was both true and comforting, and he needed comfort. Since the Mimi had heard the wind in the Watha-gun-darl's hill Wirrun had felt at every step that the Ninya were at his heels. 'Any rate,' he said, 'we know we're in the right country now. That's something.'

'A country may be large,' said the Mimi; and that was true but not comforting. It spurred Wirrun into a faster stride and made him search the dark with keener eyes; for if they were already in Nargun country he must miss no opportunity to speak with a spirit. He could not wander up and down the coast vainly searching for he did not know what.

The track was dark now that it lay between trees. He saw the Mimi's eyes turn sharply into the dark, and paused to look and listen. There was movement, a black shape low on the track; while he strained his eyes it snuffled away into the heath.

'Some old dog,' he told Mimi, who had followed it with her eyes.

They walked on. The sky had the shine of black

glass; the stars were sharp and the air crisp. The night had passed its peak. It must now have reached the smallest hours of morning. Wirrun felt the Mimi give a small warning tug on her cord. He followed her look and in a minute saw another black shape low down on the path. He thought it might be the dog again, but he saw that it waited for him. In a few more steps he saw that it was one of the little grey people they had caught in the early evening fleeing from their rocks. It was a Nyol.

'You waiting for me?' he asked, and the Nyol nodded.

'Message,' it rumbled. 'From Wa-tha-gun-darl.'

So Wirrun and the Mimi sat on the dew-wet track to bring themselves closer to the Nyol; and Wirrun heard how the ice had come to those fierce little fighters on the hill.

Four

Wirrun sat with a face of stone staring into the dark, and once or twice he muttered 'Cripes!' in pain. He was thinking of the angry men who had wanted to drag him to the bulldog ants and instead had given him water; the little men who sternly grunted 'No fire'. The ice had beaten them, but he knew it would have been a good fight.

The Mimi and the Nyol, one on each side, watched him with their old spirit eyes. This, they knew, was the curious thing that men were made for: to care. Spirits might care sometimes when something could be done. If they were the right kind they might help when help was needed. They might be and know and remember and do; but men cared even when they could not do. Only the earth itself knew what good that was—some cord that the earth had twisted and used to bind its creatures together. So the Mimi and the Nyol watched and waited while Wirrun mourned; and somewhere in the dark a dog snuffled.

At last Wirrun turned to the Nyol again. 'Four dead, you said?' The Nyol nodded.

'Under the ice,' it said. 'More soon, maybe. Skin off, all cut, all cold.'

'That's bad. That's very bad. You going back?' The Nyol nodded again. 'When can you be there?'

The Nyol's bright eyes looked at the sky. 'By morning.'

'Wish I could travel like you,' said Wirrun heavily.

'No good,' said the Nyol. 'You find First Nargun. Look here, look there, keep looking.'

'Yeah. Only don't you forget to look too; and come and tell me if you hear anything.' The Nyol nodded. 'Well, tell the people . . . tell 'em I'm sorry and I wish I'd been there . . . and we'll finish with these ice people yet. Tell 'em that.'

The Nyol nodded for the last time and vanished into the dark. Wirrun looked after it for a moment. Then he turned aside, and he and the Mimi went their own way. The track was now travelling uphill, and he made himself stride up it fast in spite of his tiredness. The Nyol's news made him feel more than ever that disaster travelled close behind; and in all this night's walking he had met only the Nyols and the hairy man-beast, and neither had known where the Eldest Nargun could be found.

'We might as well have stayed on the wind,' he grumbled, climbing faster to make up for it.

'Only by walking,' the Mimi pointed out, 'have you learnt that the Eldest is in the sea.'

'And about the Wa-tha-people. I could've done without that.'

She cat-sneezed impatiently. 'And I, I learn much about men. Their heads are hollow when their stomachs are hollow, and that is often. You must eat and sleep again.'

'I go slow enough compared to your sort without wasting the dark,' said Wirrun.

'Day is near, and there are white people. See there.'

The climbing track had reached a point where the forest broke and the ground on the left fell sharply. Looking down Wirrun could see a black depth below and hear a quiet lapping of water among trees. At first this seemed only a small coastal lagoon like others they had passed, but as he looked further through the grey dark he saw more distant humps of trees, and beyond them farther stretches of black water. This was a large and winding water threaded with land; and three far-off points of light would be some village on its shores. He remembered that they had crossed the border and thought he knew from the map what place this was. The Mimi was right: there would be more than a village or two here. At this time of the year there would be tents and cars and caravans, and all the anxious pursuit of happiness. It would be hard to find a quiet place to sleep.

'We must go round it, inland,' he said.

'It is far around this water,' said the Mimi.

'Well, we can't stop here. I need a bit of cover from hikers, or they'll be tripping over me all day. And you can't lie up in the deep rocks with the Ninya so near. We'll have to find you a hollow tree, or a big boulder on the surface, or something. We'll just have to go on a bit.'

They went on up the slope, hoping to stumble on a place of shelter and surface rocks. Soon they found they had reached the top of a ridge, and the ground began to fall. The Mimi paused uneasily for a moment, but followed Wirrun down the slope clutching her loop of cord.

There seemed to be some gully below, dark in a thickness of forest. The Mimi hesitated a second time, and this time Wirrun paused too. He could feel a clutch of cold about his ankles. They went on down a little way and stopped again. Wirrun's knees were aching with cold.

He turned and looked into the Mimi's face. It was all eyes in the dark, and he could feel her quivering. He gripped the power in both hands and showed it to her for courage. 'We gotta go on,' he whispered. 'Very quiet.'

They crept on without a sound, for the Mimi's tread was always silent and the power was helping Wirrun; and the dank chill rose around them as they went down. They paused often, and the Mimi listened tensely. Wirrun thought he too could hear a sound: a grunting and blowing down in the gully to the right. They reached the stony bed of the gully and the cold was deep and biting. The power was throbbing in Wirrun's hands; he turned down the gully towards the gasping sounds. As he turned he steadied himself with a hand on a rock and felt the bite of frost.

The grunting and blowing went on—and all at once broke upward into a howling bellow. It brought them both to a stop, for Wirrun had never heard such a sound of terror and perhaps the Mimi had. It died, yet still it seemed to fill the gully as if the forest held it or the stars threw it back. . . . But the power still throbbed in Wirrun's hand; in a moment he had to go on, and the Mimi followed stiffly.

It was lighter in the rocks of the gully than under the trees that fringed it. They could choose their way among boulders, and past hollows where water should have flowed and that were filled now with ice. They could see that just ahead the gully turned sharply. The grunting and blowing came from round that bend. They went towards it in dread.

Wirrun lifted his eyes from his feet for a moment to measure the distance, and as he raised them caught a glimpse of a black opening in the rocks on his side. He stiffened like the Mimi and turned that way as though he could not help it. He was chilled with cold already, but a new chill was creeping up his spine. He took two steps and bent to look into the rock.

A depth of darkness running back into the hill. Two twilit shapes, silent and still, white with a sparkle like salt. Green eyes glowing under needles of ice—faces of frost with green eyes colder than death. They sprang backwards like spiders into a hole; the rock was dark and empty.

Still stiffly he turned to the Mimi, and she knew from his face what he had seen. She stood and shuddered. Then that howling bellow rose again ahead, and shattered their frozen stillness. The throbbing of the power urged them on. They went unwillingly to what they knew was another terror.

They rounded the bend. There was a large pool into which the water of the gully should have trickled and splashed. Now it was locked in ice of a strange milky colour, and fringed with frozen ferns. And something was fixed in the ice.

The head was reared up as though it had been climbing out of the pool when a sudden freeze caught it. The eyes were red and rolling. Through the milky ice could be seen the darkness of a great body. Wirrun could not look at the rolling red eyes, even with the power in his hand, but he seized a heavy branch and began to smash at the ice.

It was hard and thick. He only sent a jar through all his body. 'Quick!' he gasped to the Mimi. 'A fire!'

She dropped the cord and stood afraid while he rushed for wood and sticks, and while he laid them from the bank to the ice farthest from that terrible head, and while he threw down more branches from the edge of the gully. But she roused herself and had a fire burning on the lip of the pool when he threw down his second load.

'Another one!' said Wirrun, and laid more branches in place and sprang away; and two fires were burning when he returned. Wirrun heaped them into quick-blazing bonfires. Burning sticks fell and hissed on melting ice. The great head twisted and bellowed, from the heat or the ice or anger, and Wirrun had to look at it in the new white daylight.

It was a thing of many kinds that could not be truly seen, but its red eyes were like death and its bellow was like fear. It was like a calf, like a seal, like a man, it was white, it was black. It was all these things, together and separate, in one fearful beast, and it had haunted the land since the land was young. The red eyes rolled. He knew what it was and had always known. It was Mu-ru-bul, Tu-ru-dun, Bunyip, that seized men and dragged them into water-holes or waited for them quietly in reeds; that killed and ate men, or only held them close to it till they died. Wirrun heaved up heavy rocks and hurled them on to the ice till it cracked across. The ice tipped and heaved; he sprang back with his hand on the power, and the Mimi scuttled beside him.

The monster dragged its heavy body out on the opposite bank and lay half over the rocks. It had heavy shoulders with arms, or flippers. It was feathered, or furred, or scaly. You could not tell what it was except that it was dreadful.

But it lived in water: in lagoons or swamps or rivers or the sea. And it was old and strong and very knowing.

And the Dulugar could not answer Wirrun's questions because it did not go into the sea.

And in Wirrun's hands was the power that was old and strong and knowing too.

So Wirrun spoke to Mu-ru-bul, Tu-ru-dun, Bunyip, dragging his few words out of himself.

'The land sent us to fight the ice. I gotta find the Eldest Nargun quick. They say it's in the sea near here. Do you know where?'

The Bunyip rolled its head and gazed at Wirrun and the Mimi. It did not speak. Its eyes were spirit-old, knowing loneliness and fear, so that Wirrun had to drop his own to the broken ice again. But the Mimi's eyes were spirit-old and lonely too. She looked steadily back, and after a moment whispered to Wirrun.

'The Great One is angry, for I think the Ninya have tried to take it as if it were some small thing. It may be that the Great One will seek the Eldest in the waters.' She paused. 'But I think you need not fear it.' But Wirrun thought that all things, and even the Bunyip itself, must fear the Bunyip.

Mu-ru-bul, Tu-ru-dun, Bunyip, raised its mysterious unknowable bulk and looked upward between trees gold-tipped with sunrise to the sky that had turned from quartz to opal. It turned its head and looked for a long moment down the gully. Then it heaved itself back on the tipping ice and sank.

'It's gone down under the rocks,' said Wirrun in a dazed voice. He was still shaking with cold and other things.

'Come,' said the Mimi. 'You must go out of this place.'

He was almost too cold and weary and afraid to move, and she had to hiss at him. Then he pushed his smouldering fires out on the cracked ice of the pool and began to drag himself up the farther ridge. The frost had melted and the ice would soon melt too, and the Ninya's cold was flowing down the gully and away to the sea.

They climbed slowly up into the warmth of the morning, to a leaf-mouldy ridge that carried another forest; and a little way on in the forest they found three tall boulders standing together.

'We've been helped,' said Wirrun to the Mimi. 'This is what we want, and I couldn't have gone much further. I'm beat.'

If he was too tired to go on, still he could not sleep yet; and the Mimi too still shivered from time to time. So between the rocks they made a fire to melt away their chill; and when the horror had gone out of them Wirrun felt warmed and rested, and roasted potatoes in the fire. He and the Mimi shared them, letting the fire burn down as they and the day grew warmer.

'First time we've shared a meal,' said Wirrun, burying the fire when they had finished. He expected a hiss or a cat-sneeze, but when he looked up the Mimi had vanished. She must have slipped away into one of the large boulders.

He stretched himself out between them and in spite

of his weariness wondered whether he could sleep, for he had seen the clash of two great earth-powers. He had caught only a glimpse of the green-eyed Ninya, but in the heavy warmth of the morning he was shaken to remember their cold. And they were very sure of their power: they had dared to trap the Bunyip as they planned to trap the Nargun. He wondered why they had failed to take it.

Sleep, said the land; and it folded around him the heat of its summer and the quiet of its trees.

Wirrun rolled over on his side. As he drifted to sleep it was not the Ninya that he saw, but the old red eyes of Mu-ru-bul, Tu-ru-dun, Bunyip.

He did not see a black dog that lay in a patch of sun beyond his boulders. The dog too seemed to sleep.

5

❖❖❖

In the Country
of the Narguns

One

So Wirrun slept above the gully where ice had trapped the Bunyip; and while he slept the day grew, and laid its heat over ridges and gullies of forest. In long reaches between them the sand-locked water lay still.

Yet the forest was astir, full of restless, anxious movement. There were rustlings and patterings and whispers as the small earth-spirits ran and hid. Nyols, little star-eyed shadows, fleeing out of their rocks; Net-Nets, small wild hairy ones from the caves and rock-hollows; Potkuroks from the waters, their prankster faces now woeful like clowns; they slid and scampered, driven from their homes and seeking shelter. When they met they whispered to each other before they hurried away.

'Cold wind blowing.'

'Ice comes.'

'Ice here.'

Hidden in leafy places the Turongs watched and listened. So far they were safe; they kept still and hoped that the ice might not reach their trees. And while these little earth-things scurried to and fro in fear, a great and ancient one went secretly searching for another. The Bunyip was hunting for the First of the Narguns.

It was a silent search. When the Bunyip cries it stops your breath with fear, but that is not the moment for fear. When the Bunyip hunts it hunts silently, and fear waits for the last moment of the hunt.

The Bunyip went unseen through weedy swamps and close under the banks of rivers, and where it went the

120

water was clouded, milky. It went underground into darkness along old and secret streams, by channels deeper than the ice-wind of the Ninya found. These dark and secret ways took it from one river system to the next, and to the rocky edges of the sea. For who should know the dark places better than the Bunyip? It had lived in them since the People were scattered.

Of all the ancient spirits known to the People, only Bunyip had been seen by white men too. When the forests first began to shrink and the sheep to spread, only Mu-ru-bul bellowed its rage and pain. And white men saw and heard. They questioned the People and heard its names, but names are not enough. The white men knew that there must be a word of their own to put to the names, or the thing could not be real. They searched for the word.

They collected sheets of words and argued over them. They examined the words of the People, and insulted the People's professional knowledge with foolish questionings. And while they studied so earnestly Mu-ru-bul, Tu-ru-dun, Bunyip, the mysterious and unknowable, took its anger and pain into the depths of the land. Then the white men, forefathers of Happy Folk and Inlanders, knew they had been right: that if they found no word for a thing that thing did not exist. It was proved, for here was a creature they had seen and heard, but they had failed to find the word and it had vanished.

Meanwhile Tu-ru-dun came to know the deep places and secret waters. In the quiet of dawn or dusk it sometimes came to the surface to look again on land; to feel the dizzy swing of the sky and breathe deeply of forests and suns. So it had done this morning, coming out of deep places by its own ways into a pool in a gully.

It had felt the sting of ice and thought little of that, for it met ice sometimes. Then this ice had tightened suddenly into a clutching fist, and the bellow of Bunyip shivered the gully and the Ninya fled from what they had caught. And the anger of Mu-ru-bul followed them, strangers who dared to trap it in its own country.

So now Tu-ru-dun went silently through reeds and under banks, by swamp and river and shore, in sun and in darkness, seeking the Eldest Nargun. And the Ninya, in windy caverns from which the Nyols had fled, knew nothing of this though their leader was angry.

They huddled in a sulky group in a frosty cave while he paced at the end of the cave. They could have shouted back at his anger, but they hated his scorn. They were also shaken, for they had not meant to trap a Bunyip and had never before heard one bellow. They would not look at their leader while he lashed them with sneers.

'Come now,' he said, pretending to wheedle. 'You are not children of the People but men of the Ninya. It is certain you had reason for your act; there was thinking in it somewhere. Tell me, that I may know the thinking and see the reason. Inform my ears.'

They hunched their shoulders and said nothing.

'The task was simple: to bring me a spirit of this country, that I might make it tell where the Eldest lies. Every day we see the small weak ones, helpless against the Ninya as a lizard against the People. To keep their freedom they must talk. Yet you trap a Great One, as great as the Ninya and ancient beyond speech. Why is this?'

They shuffled their feet and looked away.

'To take the Nargun we make this long journey and lay our plans with care. A Bunyip is no less than a Nargun, yet you take it in a morning's walk. For what reason?'

Silence except for the rustle of frost under shuffling toes. The leader threw out his hands.

'I ask only your reasons and your thinking! Why do you take the Bunyip? And having taken it, why do you let it go? Once the harm was done it might have been held in ice as the Nargun may. It has been angered; it may work against us; yet you ran off and let it go. What was your thinking on this matter?'

His ice-ears caught a sullen mutter; he was pressing

them too hard. They were lifting their shoulders and turning their heads; soon there would be angry shouts, excuses turned against each other, a fight or an attack on him. He changed his tone.

'Well, you have been foolish. But if you cannot tell me your reason there is one that I can tell you: your power grows strong. Now you have hope and the ice builds fast, it grows in a moment. You had caught the Bunyip before you knew it was there. That is the Ninya's part, to build the ice, and now the time has come to build a little. Let us find a high ridge looking down the shore, that the Eldest may see it from far. Let us make it a wonder of snow and ice to bring the Eldest against us. We shall see you trap a Nargun as quickly as a Bunyip.'

They did not shout or chant, as on a morning when they had not caught a Bunyip and heard it bellow, but their sullen faces lifted and they went on through the caverns looking for branches that ran towards the sea. Above them the forest's green roof enclosed a green-lit shade. Cicadas sang, a sharp vibration of sound at the edge of silence; farther away the sea hushed and dreamed; and from here and there about the inlet came the sounds of Happy Folk on holiday.

Cars laboured over bush roads, moaning to their caravans. Power boats hurtled across silent reaches and howled to their water-skiers. Happy voices twittered or lowed as climbers and swimmers called to each other. The summer day folded over these sounds and turned them into echoes, sleepy and soft. But as the morning grew a new note was heard in the voices of the Happy Folk.

It began in the village when the morning papers were delivered to the store. The storekeeper, small and wiry and brisk, snapped the fastenings on the bundles, tore them open and slapped the piles of newspapers on to the counter. Headlines leered up at her: NSW FREEZE APPROACHES BORDER! GLACIER AT TILBA-TILBA! There was a photograph, grey and unreadable. It was hard to see in it the tribal cave of the Wa-tha-gun-darl, or the Ninya's cruel wall that had shone and glittered by moonlight.

The storekeeper bristled and reddened with shock. The last report of frost had been almost a week ago and far away safe to the north. Suddenly she was offered a great block of ice only a hundred miles or so from her counter. It was too much to believe.

'A disgrace!' she snapped fiercely. 'It ought to be stopped! Right at the beginning of the season, too! How do they expect us to make a living?'

The carrier paused in his unloading of cases and came to lean on the counter and read the headlines. He whistled. 'Looks bad.'

'It's downright wicked, that's what it is, making trouble and taking the bread out of people's mouths. And if that's supposed to be a glacier I'm Queen Elizabeth. These papers are all the same—always stirring and looking for trouble. Anything to be controversial.'

'Well . . .' said the carrier, frowning. 'They wouldn't hardly make a great block of ice and take it up there to take a picture, I don't reckon.'

'*Don't* you? I wouldn't put it past them.' She gave the pile of newspapers a ringing slap. 'Hearsay, that's all that is. And never mind what it does to the tourist trade that they're always on about. They ought to do something.'

'Still,' said the carrier, who was a peaceable and optimistic man not directly involved in the tourist trade, 'this Tilba-Tilba's well over the border. I don't reckon we'll be troubled.'

'A thing like that's bad for everyone,' said the storekeeper roundly, but she brightened a little. 'I don't know what they think they're doing in New South Wales, but they can keep it on their own side of the border. We don't want it here.'

During the day the pile of newspapers went down and the news was carried abroad. Sunburnt people in shorts and bikinis discussed it in boats and bars, on beaches and in the bush. Since these were the Happy

Folk it went without saying that they split into factions, and that each faction made fun of all the others.

One faction, mainly consisting of young people, made a holiday game of the mystery and went about in groups searching enthusiastically for ice. Not finding any, they began to map 'low temperature areas' and 'isotherms', exchanging news and theories when they met each other. Stores in all the towns and villages sold out of thermometers, and caves became very important. It was a great happiness to know and visit more caves than anyone else.

A small and gloomy faction searched their consciences instead of caves. What had they done—what had Man-Other-Than-Them done—to bring this trouble on the land? They sat in small worried groups reminding each other of all the disasters caused by Man. There were enough of these to keep them happy and make them feel better than other people.

By far the largest faction loudly refused to believe in the ice in order to make it go away. They laughed a great deal to prove that the ice was not there, and made jokes about the other factions. They quoted experts of all kinds: the Weather Bureau, physicists, psychologists, statisticians. They were not to be fooled by anything the newspapers, or the land itself, might say.

The Happy Folk who ran caravan parks and motels and stores, who hired out boats and cars and organized tours, also fell into factions. Most of them were silent, tight-lipped and disapproving. They refused to talk about ice to any of their visitors, even those who hoped to find it. They knew what they wanted of tourists, and it was not to go about excitedly looking for disaster. To go where they were supposed to go, to spend what they ought to spend, and to enjoy it without making fuss or problems: that was what tourists were for. The owner of one caravan park turned a young couple out because they claimed to have seen ice in a gully that very morning. They said they had gone for an early walk and had come upon a pool where melting ice floated, and charred wood as though someone had lit a fire.

'There's been a mistake in your booking,' said the owner of the caravan park. 'The place has been let from tomorrow. To people who won't go round spreading rumours and upsetting others.'

But some of the people in the tourist trade made the most of the ice. Tours of the Tilba-Tilba cave were arranged. Service stations selling ice kept special bags labelled 'From Tilba-Tilba', and sold them to the happy unbelievers who made a hit with them at their next parties. Some motels advertised in the papers: SWIMMING OR SKIING? EITHER WAY YOU CAN'T LOSE. It set a note that a great many Happy Folk adopted.

But no one tried to listen to the land. No one had room in his mind for a big and terrible ice, or left a quiet place there for waiting and seeing. Only, in a town not far away, an Inlander named George Morrow wondered and waited. He had brought his tractor to town for repairs, and when it was done he would load it on the back of his tabletop truck and take it home again. While the work was done he worked slowly through the list of shopping his wife had given him, and listened to the Happy Folk arguing about the ice.

Since he was an Inlander he knew the size and realities of the land. He had narrowed his eyes over the first news of the ice and had followed all the reports with care. He had read all the Happy Folk's arguments and accusations, all their angry demands or glib explanations, and thought that as usual they were missing the main point. The main point was not that the ice was possible or impossible, an insult or a joke, caused by man or flying saucers, good or bad for the tourist trade. It was something more direct and simple, something a child of four could understand. The main point was the ice itself. Ice, frost, snow, cropping up again and again along a traceable route in a hot summer.

When George Morrow fixed his passive gaze on the main point, one or two other things could be seen. First, that he did not understand anything about it; second, that neither did anyone else; and third, therefore, that there was no point in any of the argument. Only two things could matter, as far as George could see. One would be a serious attempt to find out about the ice, and that might take twenty years. The second would be to find someone who did understand: someone who knew things that Happy Folk and Inlanders did not.

So George Morrow, watching and wondering, waited for those two things. And the forests and waters brooded under the sun; the small earth-creatures scurried through quiet places and the great ones went steadily on their way; the Happy Folk buzzed excitedly, and Wirrun of the People slept between the rocks. And in the hot noon, when the silence was sharp with cicada-song, he woke because he had slept enough.

Two

Wirrun woke between the rocks because he had slept enough. It was the first time since his journey by train that he had wakened for such a reason, and he was confused. He lay still for a moment, feeling for the day and the hour and the country; and when he had found them he turned his head quickly to look for the Mimi in case she had wakened him with leaves.

She was sitting on the summit of the tallest boulder dangling a dead bushrat by the tail and staring with cold dark spirit-eyes at a dog that lay beyond the boulders. It took no notice of her, whuffling in its own hair after fleas. Wirrun wondered whether it had displeased the Mimi by competing with her for the bushrat.

He asked, 'Do you want to eat that before we start? I thought we might get on a bit by daylight and eat when it's cooler, but suit yourself. We can find our way round this water after dark, there's bound to be paths.'

She blinked, for she had not expected Wirrun to postpone a meal. She examined the bushrat for a moment and lowered it to him. 'You will carry it on your back.' She watched him roll and fasten his pack, the bushrat in a paper bag in one pocket. 'I have seen many spirits,' she told him. 'Nyols from the rocks, and many small ones. They are much disturbed.'

'I s'pose they would be. It's most likely solid ice down under here.' He sighed with worry. 'We don't get ahead much, do we?'

'One greater than we two has gone ahead. We follow.'

'H'm. Hope you're right. Well, let's have a look at the way.'

In spite of what he had said to the Mimi he wanted to clear the inlet before dark. At night, even at full moon, they needed a road or track for speed; and in these forests and ridges tracks would be long and winding. By day, with only a sighting now and then from the higher ridges, he could take his own line: across ridge and gully till they passed the head of the inlet, and then directly back to the shore.

This forest journey was a delight to the Mimi. Walking by the sea where the wind waited she must stay in reach of the power, for there was no refuge in rocks where the Ninya travelled. For days she had been tied to Wirrun's belt by her loop of cord, and that was no way for an earth-spirit to walk. Here the day was still, the forests deep and sheltering. There were surface boulders, thickets, hanging vines. If wind came it must sound a warning in leaves far off: she would have time to reach shelter. She walked spring-kneed and free, keeping her distance from Wirrun and enjoying it.

Now and then she would let herself be hidden by thickets or curtains of vine. Her round eyes gleamed with a wicked red light when Wirrun stopped to look anxiously about. Seeing this at last, Wirrun hid a grin and lost sight of her as often as he could. It was not hard. Her stick-insect shape vanished easily in the forest, and he had walked too long with the Mimi at his belt not to miss her.

No hiss of leaves sent her springing for safety. The only thing that seemed to upset her was the coming and going of a dog that travelled with them. It was the black dog that had scratched for fleas outside their circle of rocks. It took very little notice of them, running on its own trails through the forest nose down and tail half curled, but crossing their path every now and then. If Wirrun spoke to it it glanced at him with its mind on other things, flicked its ears and moved its tail a little, and went on with its trailing. Yet the Mimi watched it uneasily.

They were taking an easy way into a gully by following a wallaby trail when they heard human voices a little way down the slope. The Mimi stood still, watching Wirrun. He moved quietly off the track to a point where he could look down the hillside. A group of young Happy Folk were there, crouched under an overhanging rock. They were bending over something at their feet and arguing about it.

'It doesn't count,' one of the girls was saying. 'If this gets any sun it's only for half an hour or so in the evening. Of course it's cooler.'

'We're not making value judgements,' a young man retorted. 'We're plotting an isotherm. For all we know it's just the sort of place that gets iced up: a place that only gets a bit of sun in the evening. Put it in.'

The girl grumbled and made a mark on a map. The group stood up and moved off round the brow of the hill. Wirrun watched, frowning. If the Happy Folk were making a game of tracking the ice he felt sure it was going to be a nuisance. There was little enough time to spare without dodging excited groups of young explorers or rescuing them from frozen pools. When the ancient Bunyip commanded rescue, that was in the war against the Ninya, but the Happy Folk were not part of that war. He wished he could evacuate them all to good safe homes in the inland. He was about to turn back when he saw a movement under the overhanging rock.

Two small hairy earth-things stood there looking harassed. They were watching the young people out of sight and waiting for their voices to die. Wirrun had not seen their kind before: hairy little grey people with claws. He held up the power and called to them, side-stepping down the hill. They jumped, looked about in a hunted way, then fixed him with eyes like those of the Mimi's bushrat and waited. The Mimi came up with Wirrun as he reached them.

'The ice is coming,' said Wirrun, as if it were a password.

'Ice here,' they said hoarsely.

Wirrun nodded. 'But a big ice is coming, over the land. I'm looking for the Eldest Nargun, to fight the ice with fire.'

They still looked at him steadily. 'Ice here,' they said.

'Do you know where the Eldest Nargun is?'

Their eyes darkened with awe and turned away. Their hoarse voices muttered, died away, muttered again. 'That Great One . . . very big, very strong, very old. . . . That very great Nargun, that First One. . . . Not here.'

'You don't know where?'

They shook their heads and sidled off, and he let them go. From under the rock a headline was glaring at him: a fresh-looking newspaper lay where the young Happy Folk must have dropped it. He knew now why they played their game of hunting the ice. He did not pick up the newspaper, for it had nothing more to tell him. It would have no news of the fierce little fighters of Tilba-Tilba, if they recovered or whether they mourned more dead. It had not told the Happy Folk how the Wa-tha-gun-darl defended them and their land. Wirrun thought of them in silence as he and the Mimi went on down the hill. It was some time before he noticed that the Mimi seemed troubled.

'What's up?' he said then.

'The small hairy spirits,' she said, puzzled. 'Many passed while you slept. They are called Net-Net. They are not true rock-spirits: they live not in but among rocks.'

'Well? They didn't know much, did they? Just little blokes, not likely to know much.'

She cat-sneezed at him. 'When the belly is empty so is the head. You said to them that the ice is coming and they answered that it is here. Yet they do not live in the rock where the Ninya travel. Where have they seen the ice?'

'They've been talking to the Nyols. You said there were a lot about.'

'You said to them that a great ice is coming over the land, and they answered that it is here.'

Wirrun stood still and looked at her, frowning. 'Well, it isn't, is it? You can see that.'

'I cannot see over all this country from where I stand,' snapped the Mimi.

Wirrun said heavily, 'It's getting a bit much. We'll keep the Net-Net in mind. But we can't do more than we're doing, so let's get on with it.'

They walked on. The black dog came out of the forest to sniff at Wirrun's heels. The Mimi hissed and retreated into the lower branches of a lillypilly.

'Go home,' said Wirrun sternly to the dog. It gave him an absent-minded look and a half-wag of the tail and continued to mind its own business. He gave in because he had come to feel that its home (if it had one, for it wore no collar) might be very far away. How long had it been with them? Surely he remembered a dog on the road last night? 'It won't hurt you,' he called to the Mimi. 'Take no notice and it'll go away.'

She snorted crossly and swung down from the tree.

They climbed a high ridge with a patch of bare rock from which Wirrun could check their route. They must have cleared the inlet, for he could see over gullies to the shore. He chose a gully that would lead them down to the sea, and they headed for it through the forest. There were voices of more of the Happy Folk near at hand, but these they avoided. They were nearing the head of the chosen gully when Wirrun saw one girl alone, climbing the slope toward him.

The Mimi was hiding from him again, along the slope among tree-ferns. He paused, looking for a line that would avoid this girl too; but then he changed his mind and walked on. This girl was different, dark like himself, a girl of the People. She wore jeans and a sweatshirt, her feet were bare, and when she saw Wirrun watching she smiled delightfully. He thought he had never seen a more charming girl.

When they were close he said a cheerful hullo and stood aside to let her pass. In his mind was the question, Who is she? The girl smiled again and came on, turning towards him, but just then the black dog came sniffing along on one of its trails and pushed in front of her. She had to stand and wait for it to pass, and while she waited the Mimi too came out of the forest and stood beside Wirrun. The girl's eyes flicked aside to the Mimi and back to Wirrun.

Wirrun frowned. The girl still smiled delightfully and the dog still blocked her way, for only half a second had passed, but she had certainly looked at the Mimi. Quickly he put his hand on the power and felt it throbbing. And even then, though her smile had hardened a little, the girl still looked charming and real and delightful. Only her hands and feet were too small for a real girl—and then he saw that they had claws instead of fingers and toes. They were big strong claws. If the dog had not happened to come—if the creature had not glanced at the Mimi who was invisible to humans—would the power have saved him without his calling on it?

And still only a second had passed, and the question, Who is she? was still in his mind. He changed it a little.

'What are you?'

'Bagini,' said the earth-thing. It saw his eyes on its clawed hands and held them up and laughed. Its laughter was like the creaking call of cockatoos. 'I would not have eaten you, Man,' it said.

Wirrun gave his password again: 'The ice is coming.' The thing stopped its harsh laughter and looked dark and sullen, and he wondered how it could ever have made itself charming.

'The ice is here,' it snarled, 'and will grow.'

Wirrun glanced at the Mimi. Her round eyes were fixed on the Bagini's face. 'Where is the ice?' she asked.

The Bagini sneered. 'Where even a straw thing can find it. It hangs over this country.'

'It's your country,' said Wirrun. 'I'm surprised you don't get rid of this ice. There ought to be enough of you to have a go. What about the Narguns? Aren't there any left?'

The Bagini gave a shriek of cockatoo laughter. 'Watch out, Man! Keep away from caves and dark places!'

'Never you mind about me,' said Wirrun. 'The land looks after me, and the power of the People. The one I'm looking for is the Eldest Nargun. Tell me about that one.'

The Bagini shrugged; but while Wirrun held the power it was forced to answer and did so sulkily: 'All Narguns are old, but the First is old beyond knowing. A Great One mighty in size and in power. It has seen the land in the making and holds the secret of fire. It stands in the path of the sea and turns back the ocean from its country.'

'It must come out of the sea,' said Wirrun. 'It must turn back the ice from all the land. Tell me how to find it.'

The Bagini shook its head. 'I know only that you must go farther, south and west.'

Wirrun nodded wearily. "All right. We'll go, then.'

The earth-thing turned to go into the forest, but paused a moment. 'You follow the coast?' it asked. Wirrun nodded again. 'This gully will take you quickly,' said the creature, and the Mimi looked at it sharply.

'I know. Thanks, any rate.'

It moved off into the forest, and Wirrun and the

Mimi went steeply down into the gully. Shadowed in vines the Bagini stood, watching with sly hard eyes as they went down.

The gully was one of those deep folds between ridges, with a narrow rocky floor down which water trickled. They had to climb into it down rugged faces of rock, and when they reached the bottom the path between boulders was wide enough for only one at a time. The black dog came after them, leaping from boulder to ledge.

What startled Wirrun was the feeling of night in the gully, for the sun was only halfway to the west. But the gully ran south-east, the ridges stood high and close, and he guessed that the sun shone here for no more than an hour each day. The path was rough and difficult, slippery with damp. He wondered if darkness came here before sunset, and whether they could be out by then. He must go as fast as he could without risking a broken leg.

'Stay close behind,' he said to the Mimi, 'so you can grab the cord any time. Wind might funnel up here from the sea. If I'd known this was so bad I'd have gone down the ridge instead. Might've been tough going, but it would've been daylight any rate.'

'The Bagini knew,' said the Mimi. She was troubled again for she felt that the Bagini knew something more. Some worse danger was here than damp rocks in a poor light; something to bring that sly, waiting look into the Bagini's eyes.

Three

Wirrun led the way down the gully as fast as he safely could, with the Mimi close behind. Sometimes it was rough walking, sometimes balancing from boulder to boulder, sometimes edging along damp slopes past pools or climbing over rocks and fallen trees. From time to time the dog came pushing past, to scramble over rocks and disappear. It was startling in the poor light, but even the Mimi did not hiss. The dog had done them a good turn with the Bagini.

Sometimes Wirrun would pause to look up between rock walls to the slit of sky above, to reassure himself that it was still a sunlit sky. At those times he saw that the old land held him in its fist; he felt it close its hand on him.

They edged round a bulging wall of rock and found that it opened a dark cave-mouth to the sea. The Mimi skirted wide around this, plucking at the cord on Wirrun's belt. He glanced into the cave as they went: only darkness and the shadowed shapes of rock. Beyond, the black dog sat and rested, waiting with lolling tongue. They went on past it.

Turn, said the land.

Wirrun turned with his hand on the throbbing power. He stood before the cave and looked into it. Only darkness and rock and a stealthy withdrawal of shadows. He spoke to the shadows.

'The land sent me against the ice. Where's the Eldest Nargun, the one with fire? It's wanted out of the sea to fight the ice.'

Nothing answered or came from the cave. Only the shadows stirred. Yet the power throbbed in Wirrun's hand and he was puzzled. 'There's nothing but a great rock,' he told the Mimi.

'Nargun!' she whispered, tugging fiercely at the cord. 'Come away!' Her eyes were dark with awe, for she was a rock-spirit and to her the living rock was the deepest mystery of all. 'This too the Bagini knew. Come away.' She tugged again.

'But—hang on—if it's a Nargun it's bound to know about the Eldest! I gotta try again.'

'It may know. That is nothing to you. It is old beyond speech and will not answer.'

He gave in a little, backing away and still arguing. 'But I was *told* to turn. What for, if it's no use?'

'Stupid!' she hissed. 'Lest the Great One should crush you before it felt the power.' She hurried him on, fluttering like a twig in the wind, and the black dog followed. Fear is easily caught, and the back of Wirrun's neck prickled as they went; but when he looked back once the cave-mouth was dark and empty.

The dog now chose to behave as though Wirrun were really its master, and followed as a dog should. They rounded a bend in the gully, and suddenly it was late afternoon again, with the sun shining low over the sea ahead. The gully grew wider and shallower. Soon they came out of it onto level heathland, with the sea beyond it and the hills and ridges behind.

'There!' said Wirrun, greatly relieved. 'We got that over, and there's still time to eat before sunset. We'll be well on our way before night, and there's a good moon too.'

They lit a fire inside the lip of the gully, for privacy and for shelter from the wind. The dog lay down at a little distance to wait, and the Mimi, roasting her bush-rat, eyed it sullenly. Wirrun was surprised that she disliked the dog so much, but it was not a thing that could be helped. They ate and rested, listening to the sea.

They could not know that behind them, in the half-night of the gully, a shape had moved to the mouth of the cave; that it stood there now, humped and crooked, waiting for the sky to darken.

The young man and the rock-spirit put out their fire and found a wallaby pad through the heath. This they followed, the Mimi holding her cord again, until the track met a path that followed the line of the shore. Now they were walking south-west in the dazzle of the setting sun, with the sea on their left as it had been all along till the inlet blocked their way; with folded ridges running down on their right from the mountains farther back. The dog ran and hunted in the heath as it had in the forest, crossing their path from time to time. They met no Happy Folk on holiday, as Wirrun had feared they might. If they had been there earlier the Happy Folk must have gone back to camps and caravans and motels. There were only themselves and the dog, and back in the gully the Nargun, rocking its weight from limb to limb as it dragged its slow way from the cave.

The nearness of ridges hid the sunset, but its dazzle lay on the sea and its reflection in the south-east sky. And when the path lay across a valley's mouth Wirrun looked up the valley to mountains etched dark against crimson and gold. He had to look at them; and as the next ridge came nearer and began to intervene he had to look back, over his shoulder, to those farther mountains. It was then that something caught his eye that made him stop and turn.

'Look at that!' he said to the Mimi. 'See, back in the mountains where the sun's setting? There's a high bare face that looks south-west, about. See how it shines—it's caught the whole sunset! I never saw anything like that.'

The Mimi looked where he pointed and hissed sharply. 'You are right,' she said. 'I think you never did.' At the tone of her voice he looked again.

A fire was lit in the mountain, wonderful to see, glowing with pure red and gold. But Wirrun saw that this purity of colour was wrong, and the shadows were wrong. No other mountain shone like a mirror with such a fire, nor faded into grey and white.

'That's ice,' said Wirrun. 'And snow. Now what do I do? They've built it.' He stood helpless in the heath and stared at the far, high mountain glowing with a beauty that was wrong.

'What should you do?' said the Mimi when he had been staring for some time. 'Alone, you cannot destroy what the Ninya have built. You must bring the Eldest Nargun from the sea.'

'But no one can tell me where it is! And while I hunt it the Ninya can go on building! A whole mountain in a day—how much in a week? This Eldest Nargun better be good.'

'It has fought the ice before. Long ago it fought more than a handful of Ninya and a hillside of ice. You came for this, and did you not believe it? Have you played a children's game with the earth's old children?'

Wirrun walked a few steps, but it was no good. He had to swing round again to stand and look. 'I don't know if I did or not,' he said. 'I knew it was a big ice, and terrible; but I don't know if I knew what that meant. So fast! And what's going wrong, any rate? They weren't going to build till they'd caught the Old Nargun. Does this mean they've caught it?'

The dog came by and nosed at his heels. The Mimi said, 'The spirits knew of the ice; they knew of the Eldest of Narguns; they did not know of its capture. But to know you must search.'

'No no, *no*,' said Wirrun. 'I gotta think. This Nargun's not the only thing. There's the men too, the men from Mount Conner with the songs. Maybe I'm doing no good here. Maybe I should've waited and fetched the men.'

'You have fetched them. Do you not know they are coming?'

'I said I gotta think. . . . They'll come to Tilba-Tilba because that's in the papers now. Will this be in the papers? It's a lonely bit of coast, and that's one slope in the middle of a lot of others. Who's going to see it?'

The Mimi's old eyes searched the hills. 'It will be

seen only from the coast, but far along that. It might have been chosen for this.'

'Far along the coast and out to sea. . . . Well, someone's going to see it pretty soon, even if it stops where it is. Sooner if it spreads. I reckon the men'll come on here . . . only when? It takes a time for the papers to find out and print things. Any rate, I'm doing no good going on; I reckon they've caught the old Nargun. What else are they building ice for?' He dropped his pack on the heath and sat on it, frowning. The dog went by, trailing a wide circle round them.

With the dark eyes of the People, and from under the heavy brow of the People, Wirrun watched the fire on the mountain dying. The high, twisted line of the range was sharp against the gold sky. A dark drapery of forest fell over the claws of the ridges. Behind him the sea poured over and over on to the edge of the land.

Free me, for I must be free, said the land.

'I'm doing no good here either,' said Wirrun. 'I only know one thing to do.' He stood up and lifted his pack. The Mimi took the loop of cord again and walked with him.

The world darkened; only the sky still glowed. In from the sea came a flight of great white birds, screeching and wheeling over land high up in the red-gold light.

'Not hawks,' said Wirrun, his eyes drawn to them.

'They are the bird-spirits, the Yauruks who hunt whales,' said the Mimi.

The Yauruks swung towards that mountain whose fire had become a fading glow. Wirrun and the Mimi watched until a ridge had hidden them.

The path through the heath ran into others, and those into each other, and at last into a road. The heath turned into grassy slopes and thickets of trees. The dog came and went. Evening turned to night and the night was bright with moonlight. Wirrun found himself turning often to look into the moonlight. There was a sense of watchful waiting and of movement in the shadows. He thought that some of the shadows had a shape: now a long-armed stooping shape that looked hairy in the moonlight, now a shape like a slender, graceful girl, once a blunt-muzzled rock-shape, squat and stealthy. These shadows watched.

'There's others here,' said Wirrun at last to the Mimi.

'They were always here,' she answered. 'We and not they are the travellers.' But Wirrun felt that the others travelled too, a company of shadows who journeyed with him.

He felt them most strongly in the scrub, for there all was shadow and the moonlight only made the shadows blacker. There he grew heavy with foreboding and in a little while found it hard to go on; step by step he walked with coldness and dread. Something pressed against his leg, warm and solid and quivering. Startled, he bent to touch it; it was the dog. It walked with him, close against his right leg.

On his left the Mimi spoke softly: 'We are one too many. A third walks with us.'

He thought for a moment that she meant the dog, but then he knew that beyond the dog something tall walked with them, close in darkness. He closed his hand on the power, but the coldness and dread stayed. He half-turned to the shape on his right, but the Mimi spoke quickly.

'Ask it no questions, only hold to the power. This one is not of the earth. It must be spoken to with care in the right way.'

'What is it, then?' whispered Wirrun.

'A Mrart. The spirit of one dead. It has evil powers, but you are protected. Walk on.'

They walked on in silence with the Mimi on Wirrun's left and the dog on his right. He kept his hand on the power, and the tall cold darkness walked with them. They reached the edge of the scrub and went forward into moonlight. A shifting of shadows followed, but the Mrart fell back into darkness.

'I didn't think much of that,' said Wirrun. The dog sat down to scratch fleas.

They all rested a little in the moonlight, listening to

the one long word that the sea spoke over and over.
Then they went on, close to the restless silver sea or
farther back among trees as their road led them. Wirrun saw that the coast, which had been in two minds
between south and west, now tended strongly west. He
remembered Ko-in, far away north on another mountain and it seemed so long ago.

The coast was running almost due west and the
moon reaching down to the western sea when their
track ran down the bank of a river and stopped. There
was no bridge or crossing in sight. For once they had
been trapped, by a track that pretended to be a road.
They turned north along the bank of the river in search
of a crossing.

'We could waste a lot of time this way,' said Wirrun.
'If we don't find something soon we'll have to take to
the water.'

The river lay wide and sleek in the moonlight, its
banks shadowed by reeds and trees. The dog went nosing through long grass down the bank, and Wirrun
heard it splashing at the edge.

'Better have a look,' he said to the Mimi. 'Low
tide—might be shallow enough to walk across. You
hang on to this tree while I go and look.'

He went down the bank, narrowing his eyes to look
for the dog in the moonlight. He thought it was standing in shallow water: if that went far enough he supposed he might carry the Mimi across. He sat down by
a bed of reeds to take off his shoes and try the depth.
He could not see by moonlight that the water near the
bank was clouded and milky.

Something heavy moved in the reeds. Red eyes
glinted, strong jaws clamped and pulled. Wirrun yelled.
The water rocked and gleamed as he was pulled under
it.

The Bunyip had him.

Four

From habit Wirrun had clutched the power as those great jaws closed on his belt from behind. After that he did not clearly know what was happening to him: whether he was held by the power or by the Bunyip, whether he was carried under water or on the surface, whether his eyes were open or closed. Only a few things could he ever remember about that time: his own helpless stillness like a chicken in its shell; the inescapable strength that folded itself round him and bore him; the flutter of flowing water against his skin. And one other thing, a smell: of iodine and slime and decay, but mostly of age.

He did not know for how long he was carried, or how fast, or by what route. He thought it was sometimes in moonlight but mostly in black dark. It was moonlight when his senses revived for a moment and he found himself lying in shallow water near the mouth of a river. The Bunyip snortled and snuffled, sinking out of sight; then it was gone.

Wirrun raised himself on an elbow: he was lying on the shore of an inlet with his pack beside him. Across a stretch of quiet water he saw rocks and a constant leaping and dancing of waves. He dragged himself up the beach and lay dazed, but strangely warm and dry, till the Mimi found him.

When she had heard his yell and seen him dragged under the water, the Mimi had not wrung her hands or cried out in any distress. First she had felt for a wind. Finding none, she had climbed high into the tree and watched with round, cold, spirit-eyes. She saw what had taken Wirrun, and watched it up the river. She looked at once for the black dog: it was following up the bank. She looked at the clouds and the moon. Then she climbed down from the tree and considered the Ninya.

The Ninya were building ice on the mountain. Therefore the rocks on the coast would be safe. The Mimi found the nearest rock, blew on it, and disappeared into its winking dark.

The rocks easily took her to the coast and under the river's mouth. She travelled spirit-fast along the coast, sighting often from high rocks, watching always for the dog. It was certainly following Wirrun and she knew it must come to the coast, for she had no doubt of the Bunyip's purpose in carrying Wirrun off.

Her dark possum-eyes, trained in the darkness of rock, saw as only a Mimi could by moonlight. She saw the dog from time to time and tracked it for ten or twelve miles along the coast; and she saw much more than the dog.

She saw the possums themselves in their treetops; and the drifting shapes that journeyed in the shadows, still following Wirrun in their own ways and by their own paths. She saw one great lumbering shadow that rocked from limb to limb, that seemed to travel inch by inch yet travelled fast enough; and when she saw that shape the Mimi shivered. Once she saw the Yauruks fly over crying, their great wings turning from dark to silver as they banked in the moonlight and flew inland again. She watched them with questioning eyes, for she saw that they were one fewer than when they had come from the sea. Once, looking north along a ridge, she saw a mountain that gleamed as brilliant as the moon. The ice had not grown, she saw; it lay on that one mountain still.

The Yauruks that flew and cried in the moonlight had learnt the true dread of the ice. They had feared it before as a terror from old times; but for ages now they had seen snow come and go on the mountains and remembered no ice worse than this. When, turning home from sea, they saw that mountain burn and gleam they saw only its beauty. Calling to each other in wonder they flew to the ice and circled over it, shrieking. So, full of joy, they flew into the Ninya's net of cold.

The Ninya watched with cold green eyes. A change had come over them. A few hours ago they had fumbled: they had foolishly trapped an ancient one and let it go to take revenge. But now they had built their trap for the Eldest Nargun.

They had gripped a mountain in ice and feathered it in snow, seen it glisten blue and green in the sun and turn to fire in the sunset. They had painted the delicate patterns of thaw and freeze; they were stronger and surer. They did not fumble now. At the right moment they curled a draught of cold round one of the Yauruks and drew it down.

It came falling like a spark, red in the sunset, into the cold and dying fire of the mountain. The others shrieked, hovered, and flew shrieking away. Later they flew back, calling and crying and searching, only to sweep off again in terror. And so they came and went all night, their wings black and silver by moonlight.

The fallen Yauruk plunged into a snowdrift, numbed and helpless with its wings lying limp on the snow. Now it had fallen out of the sunset and there was no fire on the mountain, only a white cold and a fading light. The cold gripped and tightened till the Yauruk gave a hoarse quark of pain. It saw green eyes above it, watching. The men of frost stood there, the Ninya. One of them spoke in creaking words.

'When will you feel the sun again?'

'Sun—' quarked the Yauruk.

'When will you reach for the wind and fly back to your people?'

The Yauruk's wings trembled on the snow as a dog's paws tremble when it dreams of cats.

'You must speak before you fly. Tell us what we ask.'

'Can't speak,' cawed the Yauruk. 'Choking.'

The white sparkling figure moved its hand and the

others drew back. The cold that gripped the Yauruk loosened a little: it breathed more easily, and after a time lifted its head and folded its wings around it in the snow. The tall white Ninya watched under heavy brows.

'Do you know the Eldest of Narguns?' it asked at last. 'The most ancient of Narguns, the one with the power of fire?'

'It calls up no fire now,' said the Yauruk, shivering. 'It crouches in the sea.'

'In the sea?' The Ninya's green eyes sharpened and narrowed. 'Where in the sea? Do you speak with knowledge or pass on the tales of others?'

The Yauruk shook its wings impatiently and jerked its head. 'Is the sea not our business? Do we not hunt and herd there? No one knows which rock is the Nargun. It has crouched among rocks from age to age till all have forgotten which is the Ancient One. But the rocks, and their place on the shore, we have always known.'

'Then,' said the frost-man, watching sharply, 'you must show us the place. Or you will never fly in the sun again but see it only through ice.'

'And if I do not fly in the sun,' said the Yauruk irritably, 'I cannot show you the place. There are those who would ask for help more politely.'

The leader of the Ninya frowned. 'And there are those who would refuse it when the ice-builders ask. You are no fighter, my friend. You love the ice?'

The Yauruk was surprised. No such question had occurred to it, and it thought little of it now. 'I know ice and snow,' it said shortly. 'Pretty stuff, but not for lying in. Unfreeze me and my people and I shall circle in the sky three times above the Eldest Nargun. You may see us and be answered.'

'That will do well. But there is no sun now. Night comes; and by moonlight one rock or one Yauruk looks very like another. You shall wait here, and the snow shall make you a warm nest for lying in. Tomorrow all questions will be answered.'

The Yauruk flounced its feathers but it did no good.

That night it stayed a prisoner in the snow while its people swept over and away; and it saw them and heard them calling as the Mimi did.

The Mimi, seeing the glitter of ice and the Yauruks crying over it, noticed that one was missing; but she had no time to brood over these signs or wonder what they meant. She read no warning that the Ninya might have won their race for the Eldest Nargun; there was only a little uneasiness at the edge of her mind. The Mimi's part was to help and support Wirrun of the People. She watched for the black dog that was free to run without fear of the wind and to track Wirrun; and she followed along the shore as it directed.

The moon dropped behind the mountains, and in a grey light from the sea the Mimi looked from a headland of rock along the coast. She saw a long beach with the low tide surging in and out, and beyond it another headland above a broad shelf of rock that the sea fringed with foam and spray. She looked landward, and saw that between herself and the rocky shelf a hidden opening led into a long inlet; and on the shore of this inlet the black dog was nosing at a long dark shape. The dog had found Wirrun. While she watched he sat up as if he were waking from sleep, and half patted the dog and half pushed it away.

The Mimi travelled the last stretch in a flash. By the time Wirrun had recovered his senses and could look about with seeing eyes the dog lay at its usual distance on one side of him; the Mimi sat on a rock on the other side, staring landward.

He looked at them in the grey light with the sound of the sea in his ears, and he could hardly believe in either of them. He was still dazed with the power and speed of Bunyip; the smell of slime and age was still in his nostrils, and his skin remembered the silken plucking of water. That the dog should have followed after Tu-ru-dun—that the Mimi should have come over wind-bare country or through Ninya-haunted rocks—this made his adventure feel for the first time like a dream. Then he saw the intentness of the Mimi's stare, with something like fear in it. He put dreams aside and asked a wakeful question.

'What's up?' said Wirrun, following the Mimi's stare. There was only a rising shoreline of grass with a shadowing of trees behind.

'Close your hand on the magic,' she whispered. 'One comes from the trees.'

He held the power and felt it throbbing, but he could see nothing but shore and shadows—and movement, a stealthy stirring, in the shadows. And at last he saw that what moved was rock: a great rock, moving stealthily under the trees. As he looked he saw for a moment a beast, squat and crooked on stumpy limbs, with dark eye-shadows and a rough blunt muzzle.

'It's the one from the cave,' he whispered. 'A Nargun.' The Mimi nodded, staring.

The monster moved forward again, stiff and old and slow. It seemed not to see them, though the dog went towards it with raised hair and Wirrun held his breath. The Nargun only gazed with empty eyes beyond the inlet, out to the rocks where the sea foamed. It lifted its blunt muzzle and gave a cry: *'Nga-a-a!'* There was no other sound while that cry lay over the sea. The leaping waves stood still, there was no breathing, till the cry faded.

The Nargun waited till then. It waited till the sea sounded and a bird moved and Wirrun stirred. Then it drew secretly back into the shadow of trees. Nothing had answered it.

The Mimi watched dark-eyed and still. Wirrun waited until she stirred, then whispered, 'What is it? What does it want?'

'Hold to the magic,' she whispered back. 'It calls to the Eldest. It cries out, one beast to another.'

Wirrun faced her. He looked stern, but the Mimi knew the eyes of the People. 'The Eldest?' he said tensely. 'Out there?'

'Did not the ancient one of the waters bring you here? Your journey ends at this place. The First of the Narguns is among those rocks.'

Wirrun turned his gaze to the tossing of foam and spray beyond the inlet. Which rock? The light warmed, and he could see them at the nearer end of the shelf. They stood humped and crouched and jaggedly erect, leaned one to another or loomed alone. There was a day's work out there to search and watch among them, and then perhaps another day's.

There was a peach-gold light in the eastern sky, and a single cloud lit up. The sun was coming. The rocks stood dark and mysterious against this light. Which rock?

'And the tide's coming in,' said Wirrun. 'It'll be pretty wild out there when it's high.'

'And look to the hills,' said the Mimi.

Wirrun looked. The massed darkness of trees and nearer ridges hid most of the hills, but there was a glimpse of farther hills with gold on their eastern slopes. One of them flashed with fire.

'The ice,' said the Mimi. 'Whatever moves on these rocks here, the Ninya may watch it.'

'I gotta think,' said Wirrun.

She nodded. It was time for thinking, and after that for eating. She moved quietly away, throwing the dog a dark look as she avoided it, and began to make a drift-wood fire.

Wirrun sat gazing at the rocks. The sun rose, sending its light along the coast, and the eastern side of each rock shone so that they seemed to face that way. A flight of great white birds came down from the hills and circled above them, shrieking. He recognized them: they were Yauruks. The Mimi watched them uneasily and saw that their number was whole again, but Wirrun did not see her frown. He watched the Yauruks circle again and again, and fly off to sea. Then he gazed at the rocks.

Which rock? They stood on guard together fronting the sea, but one had movement and a hidden beast-shape; one was a First Thing, and had seen the land in the making, and was mighty in size and power and held the secret of fire. How would such a one receive Wirrun, a stranger, with his little power that it had seen in the making? Were there songs he should know? Ko-in had not said so; but Ko-in had confessed that he was no teacher and had put the power into Wirrun's hands. And what else had Ko-in said? *I have said everything, for I have said that there must be the People.*

Wirrun stood up and stretched and looked for the Mimi. She was sitting by her fire, absorbed in it as she always was since her long days without fire. He walked gratefully to the warmth and sat beside it too. He was cold—yet in spite of his journey with Mu-ru-bul he and his pack were both dry. The Mimi had nothing roasting on the fire, and the pack yielded only potatoes. He put enough for both in the coals.

'Just as well the journey ends in this place,' he said wryly. 'But we'll be all right soon. When we've eaten we've gotta go and find the People.'

'More People,' said the Mimi. 'Have you not trouble enough with People?'

'Trouble is right—I oughta be at Tilba-Tilba to bring those People here, but I gotta go to the settlement down the coast and fetch those People to the Eldest. There oughta be two of me. Only there's not.'

'The ice does not grow; the first People will be in time. And for the Eldest of Narguns, do you not have your power?'

'I'm not a man to use the power right, not for the big things. And the Eldest is a First Thing, and there might be songs. Any rate, while I look for it in that lot down there the Ninya can watch me and make a sudden ice. These People might be able to go straight to it without bringing the Ninya.'

The Mimi cat-sneezed. It was not, as he thought, because she resented the People. It was because when he spoke of bringing the Ninya she had an uneasy feeling that they had already been brought.

Five

In his walkings about the country, meeting others of the People and talking to them, Wirrun had heard about much that he had never seen. He knew about the settlements in these parts, and his maps showed him the road to the nearest. It lay some way inland; they would have to find their way to it by rough tracks and across country. They set out westward, he and the Mimi walking together as they had for so many miles. The dog followed or led or tracked in the scrub, but was never far away.

Though he had thought about it and decided what to do, Wirrun was far from certain that he was right. Questions ran about like mice in his head. He did not know any of the men of this settlement: how would they receive him and his story? A stranger who came to them talking about Narguns . . . but at least they must know of the ice. Would they have seen the white mountain in their own country? He thought that the newspapers would not have news of it yet. That meant that the men from Mount Conner would not know either, and they could be near by now. He pictured them, in some truck or car battered by the long journey, reaching Tilba-Tilba and stopping there, baffled. There would be Happy Folk having picnics all over the hill, cars lining the road, and maybe a tourist coach or two. . . .

Beside him the Mimi was also darkly silent. She could not help her shy dislike of all people; she had to hide from them, even though they could not see her.

150

She had grown used to Wirrun and their quiet journey among the spirits—but now there would be many strangers and a different sort of action, by the People rather than the spirits. Her part was almost over. Added to that, she had caught another glimpse of the Ninya's snow-clad mountain and it seemed to her that it was thawing. It was strange that the Ninya should have built that large ice in one place and no farther; it was even more strange that having built it they should now let it melt. Had they built for some purpose, and was it now achieved? The Yauruks came into her mind again, and she saw them circling over the rocks where the Eldest Nargun hid.

So it was that the Mimi and Wirrun, taking a short cut through forest, had their minds on other things. Neither of them saw the nets laid across their path: nets, slyly hidden under leaves, made of bark-fibre cords and meant to entangle their feet. They did not see, but the dog saw; it was its business to see.

The dog had known what to expect, for it belonged to this country. Circling about them in the forest in search of such dangers, it came back to the path ahead of the walkers and knew it could not stop them before they reached these nets. It did the only thing it could: it ran ahead on the path and was itself entangled in the wicked nets.

Wirrun stopped in his tracks. One moment the path ahead had been clear and empty—in the next it was a leaping, twisting mesh of cord that tangled and held the dog. 'Cripes!' he cried, running forward to the rescue. Then he stopped dead again. '*Cripes!*'

For there was no black dog in the nets. Only a blue-tongued lizard scuttled through the mesh, quite free. Wirrun turned a blank face to the Mimi.

'It is a spirit-dog,' she said shortly. 'Or a spirit-lizard. It has guarded you since you entered this country, not trusting me. You must have seen.'

"Seen?" Wirrun shook his head, dazed. 'No, I didn't. Too stupid. But now I see how it followed the Bunyip.'

'It came between you and the Bagini with claws; and

between you and the Mrart from the dead, and twice
between you and the Nargun of the cave; and it led you
to the place where Tu-ru-dun waited. But what it is you
could not see, for it is a thing without shape and takes
what shape it will.'

The bluetongue lizard was now a boy of the People.
'I am Yabon,' it said. 'Often my kind have helped the
People of this country, and why should I not help one
whom the land sends against the ice? One who carries
the secret stone of earth and sky? It is true I have many
shapes.'

'I'm grateful,' said Wirrun. 'It seems you've helped
all right. What was it this time? What are all these
nets?'

'They need not worry you,' said the Yabon, 'but you
should watch. Watch always, on all sides, as the dog
did. The People of this country know the paths and the
spirits; they do not walk alone here as you did. The
Thinan-malkia, who spread nets to trap men that they
may catch and eat them, know of your journey. They
have seen the power you wear and know they may not
take you. Yet it is hard for them when you walk their
paths alone. They would not harm you, but they could
not help spreading the nets.'

Wirrun listened absently, for out of his worries an
idea had come. 'Is it true you can take any shape you
like?' he asked. 'Any shape at all?'

'Do you need a shape?' asked the Yabon with a
smile.

'I do that,' said Wirrun. 'I need another one of me.
That's if he wouldn't mind taking a message.'

The boy before him grew up at once and became
Wirrun: in his own shirt and shorts soiled by the journey and with his own pack slung on his shoulder. It was
like seeing his mirror-self standing on the path. At first
there was something a little wrong about the chin, but
as he looked it wavered as if the mirror were flawed
and became his own chin, with the right amount of un-
shaven down upon it.

'What can Wirrun of the People do for Wirrun of the

People?' asked the Yabon in Wirrun's voice. They grinned at each other.

'Do you know Tilba-Tilba?' Wirrun asked. 'The Wa-tha-gun-darl place?'

'I can find it.'

'The Nyols might help. There's a hill, and the highway going past. There'll be People coming on that road any time now, looking for these Ninya that make the ice. They come from a long way off, to sing the Ninya back home to their own caves. No more ice if the men get here in time.'

'Then the men must have help,' said the Yabon gravely.

'They can use it. They'll go to Tilba-Tilba because they'll know the ice has been there, but they mightn't know where to come next. They'll be looking for me and there might be one that knows me. I want you to be me, and bring the men on here. Take them to the ice on the mountain.'

The Mimi stirred. 'I saw the mountain as we came,' she said, 'and it seems the ice is melting. It was more grey and not so white, a small change that a man could not see. It may be that the Ninya have gone from there.'

Wirrun stared. 'Gone? What are they playing at, then? Building a big one like that and letting it melt?'

The Mimi looked troubled. 'I do not know. But it may be that they too have found the Eldest of the Narguns. The bird-spirits, the Yauruks, circled the place at first sun. It may have been a sign.'

'The Yauruks!' cried Wirrun in disbelief. 'Helping the ice? They wouldn't even talk about it!'

She looked at him sadly, for she knew that of all the spirits they had met the Yauruks had warmed him most. She had tried to explain, but how could a man understand? 'Who knows where the wind blows?' she said. 'If you too had asked they would have told you. At sunset the Yauruks flew to the mountain and came away one fewer. All night they flew over crying, and

this morning they flew again with a full number. It may
be that one was trapped by the Ninya.'

Wirrun shifted his feet, frowning. Trapped by the
Ninya, its great white wings stiff and frozen. . . . The
Yabon waited patiently, and in a moment he turned to
it. 'Bring the men to the place where we lit our fire this
morning. Any rate, it's better that way. We don't know
when either lot will turn up, but that's where the Eldest
is. We'll meet there.'

'I go,' said the Yabon, and went very swiftly. Wirrun
did not see it go. He was startled, even though he knew
how fast the spirits could travel.

He and the Mimi went on, not speaking but watching
more carefully as the Yabon had warned them. In the
daylight they saw no shifting shadows like those that
had travelled with them last night. Wherever they
looked only the silent forest waited. Yet there was always a sense of hidden eyes following.

'There's others still, no doubt of that,' said Wirrun,
and the Mimi's eyes turned this way and that.

They came out of the forest and found the road that
the map had promised. Two cars passed them almost at
once, and three more before they reached the first
bend. Round the bend they came on a party of hikers
who argued loudly, waving notebooks at each other.
The Mimi's eyes darted about restlessly as if she were
looking for a way to escape. Even to Wirrun the hikers
were more disturbing than the hidden eyes in the forest,
for those watched quietly and knew what they saw and
were part of it. He hoped that when there was singing
to be done no Happy Folk would be there to listen and
argue and wave tape-recorders.

He and the Mimi skirted the edge of a village and
followed a track to the settlement. The little box-cottages
scattered about looked like those on other settlements.
The Mimi hung back, looking obstinate and shy.

'They can't even see you,' Wirrun argued; but she
dropped the cord and stood back, and he had to give in.
'Oh, *all* right. Is there a rock or something where you
can wait? I'll pick you up on my way out.'

The Mimi gave her sneezing snort. 'I am not your digging stick that you pick up as you go. I go my own way and meet you again when I choose.'

'But hang on! You can't walk out on me yet! These blokes might think I'm mad—they mightn't want to help! We're not finished yet. We don't know what we might have to do, you and me, and how can I get on without you?'

The Mimi stood tall and thin and proud. 'Have I not brought you safely this long way, as the spirit of the mountain said? Have I not done what the Mimi cannot do? And while you need this Mimi will I leave you to a Yabon, a thing without shape?'

'Not you,' said Wirrun, much relieved. 'You're an ice-fighter. I'll see you, then.' And he walked through the gateway to the settlement, leaving her there. When he looked back over his shoulder she was gone.

There were not many People to be seen on the settlement: three or four children playing under trees, a woman coming from a garden, another leaning in a doorway. Wirrun looked for old men and saw none. There were two of middle age, sitting in the shade with their backs against a house-wall and talking together. He walked towards them. They stopped talking and sat watching him come. Even when he was quite close they did not speak, but looked up at him and waited.

Wirrun spoke politely, telling them his name and where he came from and they nodded silently, still waiting. He opened his mouth to speak again wondering what he could say to make them sure of him: how to save the time of slow consideration and take a short cut to their belief. 'You got a thing here called a Yabon?' he found himself asking.

They looked at each other and waited. So he told them how the Yabon had seemed to be a dog, and had brought him through the country and saved him from the nets of the Thinan-malkia. He made it a joke against himself, acting his shock when the dog became a lizard and a boy. And their faces relaxed and they laughed softly.

'He's a good bloke, that Yabon,' they said.

'He is that,' said Wirrun. 'He's still helping, and I can do with it. I don't reckon he'd mostly help a stranger, would he? But he knew the land sent me. They all know that now. The word's got round.' And seeing that they looked at him differently and waited to hear, he squatted on the ground in front of them and told his tale.

It took some time, even cutting it as short as he could. He left out much of the early part but told of the spirits he had met in this country, for by these they could judge the rightness of his story. Their eyes deepened when he showed them the power, and he saw that they knew it. They grinned and looked fierce when they heard of the great rock-shape from the cave and of Muru-bul, Bunyip. And at some time in the telling he saw that the two men had become ten. Several younger men and two or three older ones had come from gardens or cottages to hear.

They had not known the ice was so near and looked at each other when they heard of it; but they had known of it from farther off and wondered.

'I seen it coming,' said one wisely, and the others nodded.

They nodded again, solemnly, to hear that the men of Mount Conner were coming to sing the Ninya home; but Wirrun saw that they were uneasy when he spoke of the Eldest Nargun. At first he thought this was because he was a stranger and not a proper man, but he found that it was for another reason.

'This Eldest Nargun,' he said. 'I know which rocks but I don't know which one. And I don't know how to wake it up and make it help. It's a First Thing—are there songs for it? It's your business, this Nargun.'

They looked with shifty eyes and at last confessed that they did not know any more than he did. They were uneasy because it was their business and yet they could not help.

'These Narguns,' they said, apologizing, 'we don't make no songs for 'em, we just keep outa their way.

But that old one, now. . . .' They looked at each other, worried.

'Old Johnny Wuthergul,' said one of the older men suddenly. 'Where's he at?'

The whole group brightened at once and began to remind each other.

'He knows that old Nargun. His father told him, and his father before that. He could talk to it.'

'It was like it was their business, that family. Or they took it for theirs.'

'Up past Bairnsdale, old Johnny is, in the hills.'

'He's old, but he could talk to it.'

Now they knew what to do and were light-hearted and brisk. There was the Holden: Fred would drive it up past Bairnsdale, and Butcher would go with him to talk to old Johnny Wuthergul and bring him back. Early tomorrow, they'd be back, if someone had money for the petrol. They saw that Wirrun was worried by the loss of time and set themselves to deal with that.

There was the utility truck as well as the Holden: Percy would drive that back to the inlet with Wirrun, and the rest of the men would come too. Between them they'd keep an eye on the place, and sort of watch out for the Eldest of Narguns, till old Johnny could be brought to talk to it. They'd work out some way of looking after it. And first they'd have a good feed, and make a collection of blankets and axes and ropes and beer, and of anything else that might be useful for a night out guarding a Nargun.

They carried Wirrun off to wash and be fed while an old grey Holden, its doorsills lacy with rust, drove through the gate-way and headed for Bairnsdale.

6

❖❖❖❖❖❖❖❖❖❖❖❖❖❖❖❖❖❖❖❖❖❖❖❖❖❖❖❖❖❖❖❖❖

The Eldest Nargun

One

The Ninya's trap, the mountain-slope of ice and snow, had stood high above the coast for a day. It had risen pure and fierce in sunlight, grey and menacing in shade; at sunrise and sunset its cold fire glittered, calling a challenge to the Eldest of Narguns. But the Eldest did not come. It lay in the sea and sometimes dreamed of fire, and never saw the fierce white stinging snow.

In these days the Eldest did not look to land for it was weary, weighted with age and power. It knew the land in every grain of its rock: the molten pouring, the long twisting and shaping, the grinding by the wind and water, the hammer-strokes of sun and frost. It knew life, that warm and secret decay that crept over the land. The land was in the Nargun and of it.

Now it had set its might against the sea and the sea still rode against it. After many ages this battle was not over. It was a heavy thing to be the Eldest; to hide the secret of fire, to nurture an anemone and a coast. Sunlight lit the ripples and the shadow of a bird passed over. There came the first crash and foam of the new tide, and the Nargun spread its weight and held fast. It remembered dawn, and a cry from the shore that it answered, and this warmed it. But it did not see the mountain where the snow was turning brittle and the ice had begun to melt.

The Ninya had waited, calmer and stronger by the hour. They had waited for a great, slow power with the might and endurance of rock, to sidle from the shadows and call up red fire to destroy them. They waited to catch it in their sudden trap of ice. But the Eldest did not come.

They saw sunrise light their mountain and released the captured Yauruk. They watched a flight of Yauruks circling above a shelf of rock. Then they withdrew into twilit caverns where the wind howled again and the frost grew. They left their mountain to thaw.

Their leader was proud and boastful. 'Have I not led you well? From the far centre of the land, out to its edge and down its long coast, till we stand above the very place of the Eldest!'

'Ah,' they said. 'But why did it not come against us?'

'Who knows the ways of a First Thing? It may be that the Nargun saw the trap and would draw us down to it. No matter, for now we know where it lies. We need not wait for it to come rock-slow. We may go wind-fast and snap it in ice.'

'Ah,' they said. 'But in the sea. Perhaps we must think with another ear, for the sea is slow freezing.'

The leader frowned. 'It is slow. But the power of the Ninya has grown with freedom and use; we are few but a mighty power. Have you not learnt your strength? Let us see this place and plan with care, and in two days the land is ours.'

They nodded and thought. And while they planned, the old utility truck from the settlement rattled along the road.

Six of the men sat on the floor in the back, talking and laughing with excitement and singing snatches of songs. Wirrun sat in the cabin with Percy and Waratah, the two to whom he had first spoken. Percy drove, and all three thought in silence about guarding the Eldest Nargun until old Johnny arrived to talk to it.

The utility truck could not take the short cut through the scrub as Wirrun and the Mimi had done. It had to follow the main road through the nearest town and then find its way by secondary roads and bush tracks to the inlet. In the town they stopped to add to their mixed collection of supplies, for they had to provide for a night at the inlet with two meals and an indefinite number of snacks.

The men in the back jumped out to go in different directions: for more beer, more sausages, potatoes, butter. Waratah wound his window down and shouted after them.

'Kerosene!'

They paused to look back at him and think. The Ninya dreaded the Eldest Nargun for its power of fire; therefore fire would be a useful weapon against the Ninya. They nodded, understanding about the kerosene, and counted their money again and exchanged sums. There would have to be fewer sausages.

The three in the cabin of the utility waited for the shoppers to return and looked idly at the town. Wirrun thought it looked like an ants' nest. He found himself frowning and watching with attention: there were so many knots of people talking excitedly. Those who walked on the pavements hardly ever passed with a nod or a few words; instead they stopped and drew together like ants meeting on a trail. They were disturbed about something, he was sure. He got out of the truck and went into a newsagent's to buy the local paper.

He stood on the pavement and checked it carefully. There was no story of ice on a mountain, or any other exciting event that he could see. Yet the newsagent behind the counter was watching slyly while Wirrun read; and the nearest knot of people was silent and watching too. Something had happened: something that should have been in the paper and was not. Wirrun thought he knew what it was.

They had found the ice and snow on the nearby mountain—more of it than had been found anywhere else. They had decided not to let the news escape in case it was bad for business. It would be like the Happy Folk to keep bad news secret when they could not explain or deal with it. They would be on the watch, making trouble or playing games. Wirrun went back to his seat in the utility truck, still frowning. The eyes of the townspeople followed him. So did a pair of passive In-lander eyes.

George Morrow's tractor was repaired now. Most of his gear and his shopping was packed in the truck and now he was having the truck filled with petrol. Tonight he would load the tractor, and early tomorrow morning begin the long drive home, unless it turned out to be worth waiting for another day. News of the ice would be worth it, for when the land behaves in a wrong and mysterious way an Inlander pays attention. George Morrow was still wondering and waiting: for some serious attempt to find out about the ice, or better still for someone who already knew things that Happy Folk and Inlanders did not.

On his last day in town he saw and heard the excitement of the Happy Folk and only smiled tight-lipped. He saw a shabby utility truck loaded with the People and only thought they seemed in a brisk good humour. He saw Wirrun studying the newspaper and frowning at the townsfolk, and he began to watch. Was it perhaps odd that in this town only the People seemed brisk and in good humour?

He saw the shoppers come back with supplies, and with four cans of kerosene; and he listened and heard a few strange words about ice and fire. He did not dismiss the words merely because they were strange, for George had the great advantage of knowing how little he knew. 'If you don't know,' he would have said, 'there's no point in arguing.' So he simply paid for his petrol and waited again until the utility truck drove off. Then he drove after it.

In the back of the utility the men still laughed and sang. They noticed that a tabletop truck kept appearing and dropping back behind them, but they took no notice until it followed them off the main road towards the coast. Then they fell silent and watchful until it disappeared again, and laughed and sang all the louder in relief. A white man would have been badly out of place while the People looked after the business of the country, but the inlet they were looking for was a lonely one. They were pleased and not surprised that the truck was going somewhere else. They did not consider the fact that on these roads George Morrow could track them by their dust trail which hung in the air and hid his dust from them.

In the cabin, Percy and Waratah had also silently watched the truck and relaxed when it disappeared. Now they waited for Wirrun to give them a lead about the work ahead. Waratah had already made a suggestion by shouting 'Kerosene!' It was up to Wirrun to take it further. He could feel them waiting.

He said, 'Fires look like the best idea, all right. We want to get a look at this place; if we can put fires right round it we might keep the ice from getting through. There's one thing bothers me, though.'

They looked and waited.

'Well,' said Wirrun, 'it means keeping big fires going till the old man comes—keeping 'em up all night.'

'We got the utility,' said Percy, 'and nine men. And there's scrub close handy. We'll keep the wood up to 'em.'

'We'll do that all right. Only they'll show up for miles. Every man and his dog'll turn up to have a look, and there'll be some stupid thing. Fires out of season—danger to the public—trespass—something.'

'That bay, she's quiet all right,' said Waratah. 'Nobody round there. Lonely roads, and rough. Couple of ridges cutting her off most sides. Nobody to see.'

'Yes,' said Wirrun. 'Only you can see the ice from there. And the way that town looked, I reckon they've heard about the ice. They'll be up and down that mountain like bees in a bottle, trying to work out if it's there or not. They'll look down on the fires from there.'

The two older men thought about this. Percy made a half-hearted attempt to miss a washed-out section of the road; the ute bounced and banged; the men in the back roared and thumped with their hands reproachfully on the cabin roof. Percy said, 'Wait and see. Get more men and a few dogs if we need 'em.'

Wirrun was still worried but he supposed this was the best that could be said. He hoped that while his small army defended the land against the Ninya it could fight unhampered.

When they reached it the place did seem quiet and lonely enough, folded away among its ridges. Only one rough track ran east and west across the head of the inlet. Percy abandoned it and drove bumping over open ground to the mouth of the stream, near the place where Wirrun had lain before dawn while the Bunyip sank into clouded water. He showed them the place and they stood around it in silence, trying to grasp that their old and terrible monster had stood with them this time against the ice. Then they left Sam, one of the younger men, in charge of the ute while they walked down the inlet.

It ran south, long and narrow, bent in the middle like a bottle spoilt in the making, with a narrow mouth for the neck of the bottle. The eastern bank was low and scrub-covered, with a long spit of sand closing in at the bottleneck. The western bank was a grassy hill ending in a snub-nose of rock that looked across the narrow mouth to the sandspit opposite. It was beyond this headland that foam and spray always flew, where the great boulders stood jagged or humped and the Yauruks had circled and cried at sunrise. Wirrun and the men walked that way, along the green hillside of the inlet's western shore.

Soon they stood on the hill-top where it fell suddenly down. They could see, across the eastern sandspit, waves rolling in to a long white beach; and below a smashing and leaping of waves on a shelf of rock that reached out into the sea. The tide was coming in again. Skeins of water ran in channels over the shelf, eddied into rock-pools, and sucked away again. At the edge of the shelf stood the company of guardian rocks. The swells broke over them, were shouldered aside, came leaping between and foamed across the shelf.

'One of 'em,' said Percy, 'is that old Nargun. Which?'

Wirrun was looking straight down, to the inmost

edge of the shelf where it met the hill. 'Wonder how far up the tide comes? We'll have to go down and see.'

They looked at him. One of the younger men said, 'Can't we put the fires up here?'

'No fear,' said Wirrun. 'I hope we can do better any rate. There'll be caves through under here. Them Ninya'll just pass underneath, through the hill, and out down there to the Nargun. We won't even know they're through.'

They shrugged. There was going to be a lot of wood-carting. He saw what they were thinking.

'We don't have to come up here and then down. There'll be a way round at the bottom.'

They climbed down the hillside to the shelf. The way was almost as steep as a cliff, with sandy trails dropping between teeth of rock or past boulders draped in pig-face. At the foot was a shallow crescent of sand and then the landward edge of the shelf. This sloped down-ward to the sea. A fringe of damp driftwood, old sea-weed and shells showed the line of the high tide a yard or so out from the sand. From time to time a wash of foam came racing up the rocks towards it. The hillface, like a wall that dipped and rose again, stretched right across the shelf from side to side. The men stood look-ing at it, pointing and discussing.

'We can do it any rate,' said Wirrun at last. 'That's if we don't mind work. We can't go farther out or we'll lose our fires at high tide, but this oughta work. Four big fires, right across under the hill, should cut 'em off by land, and I don't reckon they'd try it from the sea. We could do with more fires if we had more men, but four's as much as we can manage. Better get going.'

'Not much time,' said Waratah, nodding.

They made their way back round the base of the hill, finding how near the utility might come and where they should build their wood-heap. At best they would have to carry firewood for some distance, and to the two far-thest fires a long way; but the young men thought they might find a track to the opposite side of the hill and build a second wood-heap for those fires. They went back to the utility and explained it all to Sam over a can of beer. Then the work began.

They drove the utility slowly into the eastern scrub with men scouting alongside as it went. When someone shouted the driver stopped and the men converged; there would be a log, fallen branches, or dead standing timber. The axes barked at each other and the chips flew. It was not neat axework—as soon as the timber could be handled it was loaded into the utility. It was surprising how quickly they had their first load. Three men drove back to find or make the best track they could and unload the timber. The other six worked on with their axes to have a second load ready when the ute came back.

When he heard it coming Wirrun leaned on his axe and waited. He was wondering when to detach two men to start the fires, but he had to stop and listen to the utility. There was something wrong: its motor muttered against a deeper roar. It came through the scrub with Percy driving and the other two sitting beside him, all three heavy-browed and sober. He walked to meet them.

'There's a bloke coming,' said Percy. 'Says he'll help.'

Wirrun's heart sank. He'd been waiting for Happy Folk bent on trouble or games. It seemed that it was to be games. The heavier motor came on: a tabletop truck. The white driver's face peered from under a felt hat. It was a cheerful face with settled eyes and a mouth that could tighten easily. Wirrun's eyes narrowed. The truck stopped and he went to it with his hand on the power.

'Day,' said the driver briefly. 'Thought you could use some help. Better truck for it. Good to see men working like that.'

Wirrun's own lips tightened, for in that last remark was the echo of old wars. He said, 'We can do with help if it's meant,' and George Morrow flicked a small smile. He had been rebuked. Wirrun went back to the men who watched in a hostile group.

'That's an Inlander,' he pointed out. 'They don't play games, and the truck's what we need, and there's nine of us. We could use him.'

The sun was already behind the western mountains. They accepted George Morrow, but silently. They loaded the ute a second time and sent it back, its three men to stay on the shelf to lay fires and stack wood at hand. The rest of them worked on with Morrow's truck, from scrub to forest.

The truck carried four times as much at each load, and the wood could be loaded with less chopping. It made short work of hills and rocks and rough ground. George Morrow drove it with flair, and took it closer to each end of the shelf than the utility could have gone. He used an axe as willingly as he drove and made no more double-edged remarks. If bitterness lay between him and the men of the People, for that afternoon they let it lie while they dealt with the realities of the land and shared a beer when it was needed. By dark they had built great woodheaps at each end of the shelf and had their four fires well started. The men of the People nodded their silent thanks; the Inlander nodded goodnight and drove off up the inlet. Tension broke, and the young men were noisy with laughter again and forgot to listen to the departing truck. Only Wirrun, Percy and Waratah heard that George Morrow had not gone far. They lowered their brows and said nothing.

The row of bonfires reddened the dusk, and the falling tide swept hissing out of the gloom as if it would carry them away. There was wood stacked beside each fire to last until moonlight; the tired men had time to eat and rest. They dragged a small fire from the edge of a big one and sat round it to grill their sausages. Wirrun took his chance to wander off a little way, for at sunset when the fires were new and the smell of kerosene mixed with the smell of the sea he had seen the Mimi.

She had been sitting on a boulder on the hillside, gazing with wonder at the bonfires. He went that way and sat by the boulder and waited. She was there almost at once.

'Good fires?' said Wirrun smugly.

She hunched her narrow shoulders. 'Those who make them have the right. The fires will draw eyes.'

It was Wirrun's turn to shrug. He too was afraid of that. 'I've brought you a hot potato,' he said.

'I have eaten crab,' she said with dignity, and seized the potato. As she broke it open she added, 'A crab is a poor thing.'

They sat eating together, listening to the dark beyond the fires. 'Are there others about?' Wirrun asked.

'There are many. The shadows go to and fro. The wind is loud in the rocks, and the cold comes.'

'Where will you sleep then?'

'In a boulder, as you have shown me.'

Wirrun looked out to the edge of the shelf, where black shapes stood against the shine of moving water. 'And your eyes can't see, and your ears can't hear, which one out there is the Nargun?'

She looked through the leaping firelight and through the dusk beyond. 'None that my eyes can see or my ears can hear,' she told him. 'But the Eldest, the First One, is there.'

Two

The night grew dark and cool, but the four great fires kept it back. Wirrun thought that from a distance it must look like a bushfire out of control across the hill, and he worried again. The sea rumbled angrily. The stars leaned close, waiting for the moon. The fires threw their red heat from each to each, and up in great leaps of red and gold to the stars. The dark water caught and lost the firelight.

At first the men went to and fro from fire to fire without any sort of rule, wiping the sweat from their faces and thankful for the coolness of night beyond the fires. But almost at once Wirrun, for whom this day had been long and hard, fell asleep against a warmed rock. They put a folded blanket under him for softness and left him there. Soon five other men lay on blankets, sleeping or trying to sleep, so that they could take their turns at fire-watching later in the night. Three at a time would do the work.

Up near the head of the inlet George Morrow sat watching too. He was not sure what was going on down there, but whatever it was it flowed out of the land and it ought to be given a go. By good luck, whatever George needed for a long night out was stored in the cabin of the truck, ready for an early start for home. He had simply driven to a convenient point, parked the truck in a screen of trees, loaded himself with useful gear, and trudged heavily back.

George felt as Wirrun and the Mimi did: the fires would draw eyes. There would be Happy Folk along sooner or later, importantly anxious to discover things and put them right. They would be better off minding their own magics and leaving the People to get on with theirs. George intended to do what he could.

He walked slowly back along the track, studying it and the headland and the glow of fires behind. He found the point at which, by walking off the track a few yards to the east, the first glimpse of fires and figures could be seen. Anyone who wanted to see would step aside at this point; and he would see that these were men of the People working at fires. Gratefully George put down his load and set up his own watching station.

The little folding table that Liz wanted for the tent. The big battery-lamp for outdoor work at night or breakdowns on the road. The tape-recorder for young Bill's next birthday. The exercise-book from the truck in which he kept a record of mileages, servicing, and the contract work that sometimes helped with the upkeep. He flashed the lamp and took a look at the result. It looked . . . not like anything in particular, but official. The tape-recorder was a lucky stroke. George put on a tie; it was the only disguise he had, but quite effective. Then he made himself comfortable on the grass with half a pound of special cheese Liz had wanted, and a thermos flask.

It was not yet fully dark when the sound of a four-wheel drive warned him of the first intruder. He watched headlights pricking the dusk between trees. A little later there were heavy footsteps: only one person on the track. When the footsteps hesitated and turned his way George switched on his lamp and directed the beam. A police constable, blinking suspiciously in the light. George set the lamp on the table and walked forward into its beam.

'Evening officer.'

'Evening, sir,' said the policeman. He looked carefully at George, the well-lit table, the tape-recorder. He turned and looked at the fires and the moving men.

'Quite safe,' said George. 'No fire danger down there. It's a sea-increase ceremony, probably go on all night. I'll be recording it when they get going.'

'Yes sir? Could I have your name please?'

'George Morrow. Anthropologist. And very lucky to have this chance. There'll be a lot of excitement all over the country if I can get these chants.'

'Is that right, sir? We should have been told about this, you know. It would have saved you answering questions and we could have kept you from being interrupted by sightseers.'

George hadn't allowed for that. He blinked. 'What? Didn't young Clark get in touch with you? That's bad, that is; I wondered when I saw you. When I left a week ago he had instructions, but he's new and a bit slow. You'll get a letter of apology, of course, but it's awkward now. This ceremony only happens when the stars are right. Once in about eighty-five years. That's why no one's recorded it yet. There'll be a howl if I lose it through a technicality.'

The policeman grew thoughtful. A howl was no good

to anyone. He took out a notebook and went to the table, looking again at the tape-recorder and George's log book. 'Can I borrow your light, sir? Mr George Morrow, anthropologist. Address please?' George invented an address in Perth. 'Well, sir, I'll have to report this, of course. Can I hold you responsible for the good behaviour of these men?'

'You can that. A steady lot. You could have a word with them, but you'd need to run. Once they get started outsiders aren't allowed, or the whole thing's called off and we have to wait another eighty-five years.' George looked at his watch.

The policeman stood watching the figures at the one fire he could see. It looked like work to him: no wild dancing or waving bottles. And these scientists could raise the devil.

'I'll trust you, sir,' he said.

Gratefully George escorted him into the dusk.

The next intrusion came within half an hour and from the other way along the track. It was a single car, but loaded beyond belief with a party of young Happy Folk. They all had notebooks and thermometers, and had been out to the mountain to plot isotherms. George knew as soon as he heard their voices that a sea-increase ceremony would be right up their street. He quickly carried his table nearer the track and switched on his lamp at once.

'Evening,' he called as soon as the group had spilled from the car. 'Tickets please.'

'Eh? What's this?'

'You've got tickets, haven't you?'

'No, man. We didn't know about tickets. How much?'

George did an anxious sum. 'Six dollars each,' he said crossing his fingers. Ten of them: that would be sixty dollars. Would they——?

'*Six dollars!* To look at some bonfires! What's going on, anyway?'

'Experimental black outdoor theatre and very expensive to put on. We can't do it cheaper. The seating alone—you've got to have a natural theatre like this, that can't be overlooked except from the seating area. Then there's the transport and—'

The young man in the lead raised his voice rudely. 'Anyone got sixty dollars on him to see the bonfires?' There were boos and groans and laughter. 'Sorry, man, you just lost ten patrons. Come on, peasants.'

'I'm sorry too,' said George severely, making sure. 'People have cash for anything these days, but if it's art they want it for nothing.'

There were cries of 'Nothing!' 'Sixty bucks to sit on a rock!' as the car doors slammed. George wiped his forehead. He had nearly blown that. They might well have had sixty dollars and an eager wish to see experimental black outdoor theatre with bonfires. He should have saved it for their elders. He went back to his cheese.

He reckoned he would soon be able to relax and get some sleep, for now he was counting on a conscientious police patrol to intercept most people on the highway and turn them back. At any rate, as it grew later few people would choose to leave that safe road and venture on the unmade tracks to the inlet. They were more likely to ring the police and report fires—that walloper had been a bit of luck after all. The main risk now should be from a few wanderers who might already have left the main roads and were finding their way amid the network of tracks.

It was nine o'clock before another car arrived, from the direction by which the young people had come. In the light of their own headlamps George observed a middle-aged couple expensively dressed. He took up his post and switched on his lamp with his mind working like a pinball machine. He could not tell whether this couple was likely to rush an increase ceremony, experimental outdoor theatre, or even a drunken brawl. He must play it safer.

'Evening,' he greeted them, and chuckled happily as they craned to look at the fires and men. 'Going down? Might as well be in it. A real experience.'

The couple hesitated. The man said, 'Well, I don't know if we have the time. What's going on?'

'Snake-bake,' said George.

'Snakes!' cried the woman. 'Down there? With those huge fires?'

'Sea-snakes,' said George, thinking fast. 'The fires bring them in, to the shallow water. Very rare, most of them, and all deadly. They're going to sell me a couple for my collection. Wish I could watch them handle them.'

'Why don't you go down, then?' she asked.

'Well, prejudice I suppose. If you go to a snake-bake you have to eat your share or it's an insult. Not that I'd mind in the ordinary way, I've eaten snake often enough. But sea-snakes are the most venomous, and if they bit each other the men mightn't notice at night. Then you've had it. But it won't happen, of course. Those blokes'll all come up alive and there's no reason why you shouldn't join in. I just know enough about snakes to be prejudiced.'

'Well,' said the man coldly, 'I don't think we feel like risking it tonight either. Do you, dear?' They nodded stiffly and returned to their car.

George watched them go with a small smile. He had never before annoyed so many of the Happy Folk in one evening.

It was his last opportunity. When another hour had gone by he rolled himself in some sacking from the truck and found a smooth place to lie. He was sure it was safe now; he would have driven back to town except for the chance of meeting that same police constable on the highway. He was sure to wake up cold and stiff in a few hours. He would drive back then.

From where he lay he could still see the fires, and a cloud of red sparks that broke upwards when a log was thrown on. They were very quiet down there. They knew what they were doing, whether it worked or not. At least he'd given them a fair go.

The moon had risen. The sea writhed like a silver-black snake, always reaching for the fires and drawing back. A great grandfather of snakes with a roar like an angry king. He had told the man and woman right: it was deadly. But the men of the People faced it with their fires, and the land faced it with the huge stillness of a First Thing. George Morrow was only an Inlander, but he felt this huge stillness even while he turned on it and slept.

Around him shadows gathered and passed. They too watched where the snake of the sea coiled, where the rocks crouched and the fires leapt; where that other First Thing, the Eldest Nargun, guarded the land. The shadows drifted and watched, a gathering and thinning of darkness under the moon. They saw how the fires in their turn guarded the Nargun, where the red light fell and where moonlight lay cold. The Thinan-malkia gathered their nets. The Yauruks flew over the writhing sea after whales. The great rock-shape from the cave inched its way up the hill. The little spirits fled to the forest. The Bagini sharpened its claws with a sweet woman-smile.

The Eldest Nargun lay under the sea and felt the tide turning. It turned its empty eyes away from the moon and watched for a wavering red light on the water. It reminded the old monster of the flaming of mountains and the golden burning of the sun and the warm secret coming of life. The Nargun spread its weight against the cold drag of the sea and cried out.

The Ninya rested together, gathering their strength. 'The sea is slow freezing,' they muttered.

Three

At about midnight Wirrun woke, aching from the hardness of rock and bewildered by the red light of fires. In a moment he knew where he was and looked for the men. Three were at work, dark shapes in the red light, one bending over a fire and two dragging wood. When Wirrun stood up stiffly they made signs to each other, and the man at the fire went off to the hill and lay down. They had let him sleep past his time.

Wirrun went to bring more wood and see what was left of the heap. The Inlander had served them well; the pile of logs and branches had sunk to only half its height. There should be enough until morning. The fires were no longer leaping bonfires but mounds of glowing red that darkened into crimson at their base. They leapt into gold and flamed upward into sparks only when a fresh log was thrown on. The rock at their edges was heat-shattered into flakes. Wirrun went to stand between two fires, where men lay asleep on folded blankets. He could feel the warmth of each fire in spite of the distance between.

The heavy wood had to be dragged a long way from each side of the shelf. The men worked slowly and steadily, exchanging a few soft words when they passed. Wirrun was working with Sam and Percy. He murmured to them that the fires at each end of the row were the two to watch, for it seemed that the Ninya might slip past an outer edge rather than between the fires. But as the moon passed over and the night drew on he found himself working oftenest at one fire only:

the fire at the inner edge, where the shelf formed the mouth of the inlet. Soon Wirrun worked alone at this fire, leaving the other three to Sam and Percy. Sometimes he caught a red-lit glimpse of the Mimi, a stick-shape going from fire to fire. She had always been good with a fire.

The moon went down to the mountains and the stars swung low to the fires. The chill hours had come; Wirrun felt them in spite of the flames. The tide sent a dark wash of water to reach for the fires; it was high now and would soon be falling back. Wirrun worked harder.

The cold grew sharper. He looked to see if Sam and Percy noticed it, but their steady pace had not changed. They paused together for a moment, and above the sea's pouring he heard them chuckle. It was only here, then. Wirrun dragged logs and built his fire again into a bonfire. The Mimi came and crouched sharp-kneed in the glow to watch with round solemn eyes.

I freeze, groaned the huge still darkness behind him.

'I can't do any more,' panted Wirrun dragging another log to the fire. He worked on, and the Mimi put all her being into the blaze.

After a time he thought the cold was less sharp. The moonlight had changed too; morning was weakening it. Wirrun paused in his work and stood back from the fire. As the sweat cooled on his face and body he felt only the morning's chill. The sudden sharp cold had seeped away.

'It has passed,' said the Mimi. But still she sat and watched the fire.

Wirrun sat on a boulder to rest. He saw that Sam and Percy looked towards his fire as they kept up their steady work between the other three. Soon Percy came to the nearest fire and called a comment that Wirrun knew was a rebuke.

'Good fire, that one. Using plenty wood.'

'I know,' said Wirrun, apologizing. 'Only there was this cold snap. You never felt it?'

'Just the morning,' said Percy, going on to the wood-heap. Wirrun followed to look at the damage. The wood-heap loomed dark in the first-dawn light, and a long slow wash of the falling tide came lazily out of darkness. He had made a hole in the wood-heap on its nearer side, sure enough. He went round it to look at the farther side, and his feet slid from under him.

Ice! thought Wirrun, twisting as he fell. There was something else on the rock between the wood-heap and the water. Grimly he called to Percy while he knelt and groped in the half-dark.

The Thinan-malkia had spread their nets here. But the nets were frozen hard and lay tossed and broken.

'That ice?' said Percy's voice at his shoulder. Wirrun looked up to see him bending and feeling, and behind him Sam coming from the wood-heap.

'They've broken through,' he said in a tight voice. 'Get the men—and watch yourselves. You could break a leg here.' The cold had indeed passed, as the Mimi had said. It had passed this end of the line of fires, out to the shelf where somewhere the Eldest Nargun lay. The Ninya had won through in spite of them.

The men were coming, waking up as they ran, to look and feel. 'Who laid the nets?' someone asked.

Wirrun said, 'Others are fighting too. You ought to know which ones. Get fires started here, near as we can to the water. See you don't slip.' He was kneeling on a ridge above the water, where the sea sent long swells down the side of the shelf and through the mouth of the inlet. In the half-dark he searched with groping hands and straining eyes.

It was cold here. Channels and crevices held ice. A swell gathered ice from the rocks and floated it out to sea. He did not like the sluggish movement of the water: it should have been running out fast and strong in the ebb. And farther down where the shelf jutted into open sea, there should have been a livelier leaping as the current set that way. He remembered how fast the Ninya could work, and their cold was inside him.

Men were dragging wood towards the water or running with cans of kerosene. Three, shouting 'More wood!' had gone for the utility. George Morrow, having slept on till dawn, saw and heard and ran for his truck. Wirrun suddenly saw that in all this confusion work might be wasted, and called Waratah to help him examine the shelf.

They found pools and channels filled with ice and the edge of the shelf crusting with it, but so far one edge only. The ice started within the mouth of the inlet and followed the shelf along that side to the sea.

'If they get going here,' said Wirrun grimly, 'they'll ring us from the sea and work inwards over the shelf. We'll start the fires at the sea end and work back.'

'Those big ones, they're no good now,' Waratah pointed out.

'No more they are. Might as well break 'em up— they're hot already any rate.'

They used branches to roll burning logs from the old fires closer to the sea, and those that came dry enough past rockpools and channels they heaped into new fires. Wirrun, running to and fro with the others, saw the Mimi at fire after fire nursing each. He heard the truck's heavy motor and ran to help unload. It was a small load, offcuts from yesterday hastily gathered. George Morrow unloaded with the men and Wirrun spoke to him.

'Heard you'd stayed.'

'Thought you might have visitors.'

It was not possible that there should have been no visitors. 'You got rid of 'em?'

George grinned, heaving down a branch. 'Had to tell a few tall ones.' He looked with narrowed eyes over the shelf. 'That ice? Give me three men and four axes and we'll bring another quick one. I'm off then. Good luck.'

Wirrun called to Sam while he himself went back to the ice.

He strode along the shelf, looking inward as well as outward, slipping on glassy surfaces and saving himself, and where he found most ice he called for fire. Men ran and stumbled and shouted. All along this side of the shelf were ruffles of smoke, spires of steam, and the hissing of fire as the water got to it. And soon Wirrun

felt that this was no battle of ice and fire but a useless
skirmish, fringe-fighting. The crust of ice along the
shelf had widened; floating caps of ice had joined. He
was wasting work and wood in defence when he needed
to attack.

He remembered two green-eyed salt-white figures
glittering in a cave. That was what he wanted: to find
the ice-makers themselves, and hold them with his fires
till the men of Mount Conner came—if only they
would. He must look farther and better than he was
looking now: he must see.

He left the fires to the men and found a high ridge to
stand on, took the power of the People into his cupped
hands, and waited and watched. If he did not see the
Ninya he might perhaps see the Nargun. . . . Nothing
in crevice or rockpool, but no ice lay there yet; the sea
was drugged and heavy with ice, but men could not
stand and work on it yet; among the great rocks at the
edge of the shelf, was that a glitter?

'Mad! Blind!' shouted Wirrun. Of course that was
the place! Only those rocks were big enough to hide a
Nargun or the Ninya, and there the sea lay heaviest
with ice. And the very ice that attacked those rocks
made it possible for him to fight back, for it kept the
sea from rushing in among them. Now he could build
fires there as he could not last night—two were burning
close to the rocks already. The men must cut off all that
corner of the shelf with fires and then advance into it
with more fires. If they could only hold that corner they
could defend the old monster in it. Wirrun went quickly
back and set them to work.

Now that they had a plan the men worked eagerly.
The second quick load of wood arrived to feed their
new line of fires. They moved inside it to build again
nearer the rocks. Wirrun kept his hand on the power
and his eyes on the rocks. He remembered the stirring
of shadows, the secret movement, in that other Nargun's cave.

A Great One mighty in size and power: which rock?
Surely his fires would not anger the Eldest who had the

power of fire—but none of these men must be crushed by the monster they were all trying to save. Wirrun held the power and watched the rocks. The sun rose, and they looked at it with gold-lit faces. Beyond them the tide was at its lowest and the ice was spreading fast on the lazy sea. The men went to and fro with wood and they heard the sound of a motor.

Not the ute; not the Inlander's truck. The men from Mount Conner? For a moment Wirrun's heart leapt, but then Percy called to him.

'They've brought old Johnny. That's the Holden.'

Wirrun and Percy went back across the shelf, skirting rockpools and stepping from ridge to ridge over channels. They met the others at the base of the hill, and Fred and Butcher looked with interest at the signs of battle on the shelf and the ice in the sea. Old Johnny Wuthergul looked with interest at Wirrun.

He was old indeed, his face a powdery brown and deeply wrinkled, his hair and beard white. He had the gentle smile and seeing eyes that were common among old men of the People, but he seemed to be gently surprised by Wirrun. He said nothing until he had heard for himself what Wirrun had to ask.

'You'll see this ice,' said Wirrun. 'It's after the land. But the Ninya want this Eldest Nargun first, to freeze it so it can't call up fire against them. Can you talk to this Nargun? Tell it to call up fire and get rid of 'em?'

Old Johnny smiled. 'Where's this power they say you got, boy?' he asked.

Wirrun unfastened the power and put it into the old man's hands. He seemed to go into a dream, turning it slowly over and over. Then he handed it back.

'You want me to talk to this Old One?' he shook his head gently.

'Ice in summer,' Wirrun urged him. 'The sea's freezing down there. Fetch it out before they put a freeze on it. If they haven't already.'

'Funny thing,' said old Johnny, shaking his head.

'Can't you talk to it, then?'

The old man straightened proudly. 'My father, he

showed me. And his father before. Dunno how many grandfathers talked to it first, right back to old times. . . . But you'll wait here, boy.'

'Only there's ice out there. You could fall,' said Wirrun.

'I gotta go just me.'

'You want me to bring the men back?'

Old Johnny looked carelessly at the men and fires and shook his head. 'You wait,' he said, and went slowly forward.

Wirrun waited, for he was not of these People and the others were; but he signed to Percy and Fred and Butcher to watch over the old man. It was rough walking on that rock even without ice. He himself leaned on rocks near the remains of last night's fire and watched. He found himself breathing quickly with a thudding heart. He had come a long way for this, and it seemed to be working at last. He was glad to find the Mimi waiting near him, but neither of them spoke. They watched too tensely.

The old man went on slowly but surely, turning between ridges and pools as if his feet knew a path of their own. It was a winding path, away from the rocks where the fires were and towards the centre of the shelf. Some distance out he turned to the men who followed him, and they stayed where they were. Old Johnny went on, pausing sometimes and looking into rockpools. Beside one of these he crouched and stayed for some time; then he reached his hand into the pool and stood up again.

He turned and went slowly towards the men and fires, stood by them for a moment, then came slowly back by another path. Had he spoken while he stood and watched? Wirrun waited, tense and eager. Some of the men were leaving the fires and following old Johnny back. Words burst from Wirrun as soon as the old man was near.

'Did you talk to it?'

Johnny chuckled. 'I talked to it and I fetched it out,' he said proudly. He held out a brown-crêpe hand and opened it. On his palm lay a stone, a large pebble, the size of a teacup.

At first Wirrun did not see it at all, for it had nothing to do with the picture in his mind. When he did see it he felt as if something had kicked him hard in the middle. He could only gasp, '*What's that?*'

Old Johnny spoke warningly. 'Watch your words, boy. That's very old. That's a First Thing.'

'That's not—you sure it's the right one? *Eldest* Nargun? Greatest one ever?'

'That's right. Biggest and strongest. Been in the sea a very long time. Used itself up fighting the sea.'

The men had come up full of triumph to hear what old Johnny had done. The triumph went out of them. There was bewilderment, shame—and suddenly all the tiredness of the long hard hours. They stood in silence and looked at the pebble to avoid meeting each other's eyes. No one turned to the fires.

And the Eldest Nargun, heavy with age and power, felt again the warmth of the sun. Little wet weeds still clung to it, but the fish had darted out of them when Johnny's hand appeared. The tiny crab had burrowed under sand in the rockpool; at ebb tide the whelk and the limpet had made their long journeys to feed in the pool, and Johnny had carefully lifted the anemone from the Nargun. When the tide poured into the pool again these must all look for other shelter; they would find no Great One crouched in the pool to hide them from the sea. But the Eldest Nargun felt the warm tide of blood hidden in veins: it spread its weight on Johnny's palm and stirred a little. For a moment Wirrun saw it: blunt muzzle, empty eyes and stumpy limbs. The First of Narguns, for dread of which the Ninya had journeyed far and frozen a mountain in ice.

Yet he tried once more to prove this was the wrong stone. 'Can it call up fire?'

'Can if it wants to, boy, it's got the power.' The old man gathered a little dried seaweed, bunched it on a rock, and carefully set the pebble on it. He bent over it with a crooning sound and stood up proudly.

A drift of smoke rose from the seaweed. It smouldered for a moment and went out.

'Well,' said Wirrun carefully, 'thank you, Johnny. We saved it from the Ninya, far as that goes. Hope they didn't see it.' He floundered into silence while the old man smiled gently. What now, he wondered? He knew he should try to get the men back to the fires.

If the Ninya had seen the Eldest they would know they need not battle for it. They would slip away through caves to the mountains, leaving the men with their useless fires. Then, when the men from Mount Conner came, the Ninya would be gone and building their ice somewhere far away. But perhaps they had not seen the Eldest. Then they would lock those rocks down there in ice and believe they had caught it, and build on from there; if the men let them. He should get the men back to the fires.

But they were all tired; they ached with tiredness. Worse still, they felt foolish and betrayed, and no longer believed in the battle. Wirrun too. He had worked harder and longer than any of them for that useless pebble, and felt more foolish. And he was empty: empty with shock, and weary days and nights, and wasted work.

He had done all he could. It was up to the men from Mount Conner, as he had told Ko-in in the first place. There was only one thing left—to find some way to satisfy old Johnny, who had travelled all night to help.

And then Wirrun noticed the Mimi.

Four

None of the men could see the Mimi or guess that she was there. Only Wirrun saw her, standing like a tall stick-insect by the rock where the Eldest Nargun lay. She had drawn back a little, fearfully. Her eyes were round and solemn, full of awe. She looked on the stone and saw it whole, as she had seen the Nargun of the cave. For her this journey had not failed.

Wirrun in his weariness saw this with surprise, and then with wonder. He put his hand on the power again and saw more. Though the men stood silent avoiding each other's eyes, yet behind them the fires were tended and fed. Those strong little wrestlers from the rocks, the Nyols, scurried to and fro dragging wood from the forest. Down the shelf where the rocks stood the Nyols swarmed like grey ants and the fires burnt bright.

Among those rocks he saw that something moved: a squat and hairy figure, long-armed, creeping. The nets of the Thinan-malkia had failed but the Dulugar had come. And on this side, peering slyly between the rocks, a woman of the People smiled and sharpened her claws: the Bagini was there.

These see me true, for they are me, said the land crouching over the sea. *But where are the eyes of men?*

'Come on!' shouted Wirrun. 'We got these Ninya worried—do we want 'em to get away? The ice is here!'

The men looked up quickly, glad to hear. They were weary but they hated this failure. They wanted to be lifted out of it. They grinned to each other and strode to the wood-heap—and now the Nyols fed that instead of the fires.

Wirrun turned to Johnny Wuthergul. 'Can I hold this Old One, or does it have to be you?'

The old man gave him a straight look. 'You got the power. Go ahead.'

So Wirrun took up the First of the Narguns, the Eldest, the Great One with the power of fire, and carried it into battle with the Ninya. And his palm tingled as he held it, still damp from its rockpool.

As he went down the shelf in the early sunlight he looked over the battle. The outer ring of fires was dying and useless now, for the inner ring, closer to the standing rocks, was burning well. Yet among the rocks was the gleam of ice building fast, and fastest near the sea. The Ninya were fighting with all their strength. He saw a salt-white sparkle—a frost-man crouched between the rocks and the sea. A long hairy arm swung and the Dulugar hurled a stone; there was a grating cry, a splintering of ice, and white blood flowing on the rock. Wirrun smiled grimly and hurried on, but he was worried by the look of the sea.

It was deep at the edge of the shelf, even at low tide. It should have ruffled the shelf with waves and spray, but since first light it had lain sluggish with cold. Now it was still. The Ninya had used the low tide well to crust it with ice, and the ice extended along the shelf into the mouth of the inlet. They would need many more men to build fires all along that line; yet if the Ninya were allowed to build a base in the sea they could outflank any line of fires.

There was no time to send for more men. They must somehow attack the freezing sea with those they had. They could not build fires on it—when the sea-ice was thick enough for men to stand and work on it the Ninya would have won. Could they hurl rocks and burning logs on to the ice? It should easily crack, but the Ninya were powerful builders. They could mend the ice, crack by crack, as fast as the men could break it. If it could be broken all over—if they had dynamite, for instance—

then the pull of the sea would be released and might carry the broken ice out fast enough. The sea is slow freezing; the Ninya could hardly repair in a few minutes what it had taken them hours to build.

But there was no time to send to town for dynamite. Even as Wirrun thought this he heard cries that he knew. He looked to the sky: the Yauruks were coming. At first he could not see them but their shrieking was near. He looked lower.

They were coming on their great white wings low over the sea. Something broke the surface of the sea, something dark and shining that swam ahead. A fountain of water broke upwards. There were several shining backs and the Yauruks herded them, swooping and shrieking. The Yauruks were bringing the whales.

Wirrun stood still, full of delight. Were there three whales or four? No matter. The Yauruks shrieked and drove them on. The men stood at their fires and watched. The whales drove in, veered at the mouth of the inlet, swung aside into deep water and away. They had escaped, and the Yauruks flew in pursuit screaming of failure. But they had not failed.

The thin ice was shattered. The water, lifting sluggishly again, began to tip broken ice over its shoulder and out to sea. The men shouted and jumped about and threw more wood on the fires. Wirrun shouted too and began to run, but stopped again, still watching.

On the edge of the shelf two frosty figures crouched. They were looking with angry green eyes at the broken ice drifting out of reach . . . but near the edge of the shelf the water clouded . . . something drifted there, large and slow. A wetness of scales or feathers or fur— an arm or flipper reaching—one of the Ninya went into the sea, the other scuttled back. Wirrun caught a drifting smell of slime and age, but Mu-ru-bul, Tu-ru-dun, Bunyip, had taken his revenge and gone.

Wirrun leapt the last few yards over the rocks shouting for more fires nearer the inlet. He set the Eldest Nargun high on a boulder where men and spirits could see it and seized freshly caught branches from old fires and carried them to new. Men came and went with wood, and Nyols came and went among them. The Bagini prowled; today she was looking only for frosty men. Her cockatoo-laugh screeched—she had gouged one with her claws. The fires caught and leapt, but the ice between the rocks grew a little. The cold in there was menacing. It held the men back, as the jagged rocks held the fires back. Wirrun could not take his fires closer, for now that the sea was released it washed in and out again and would have carried fires away as it had carried the ice.

Wirrun was enraged. He seized burning branches and hurled them between rocks at the ice. The younger men shouted and hurled more. The flames sizzled and died as the branches flew: they were white with frost before they fell. The ice grew, and again Wirrun felt the cold of the Ninya inside him. They were a fearful power. Only here by the sea could they have been held for this little while.

'Behind you!' screamed the Mimi suddenly at his side. 'Up on the hill! Look back!'

He looked and saw nothing: only the clean line of the hill against the sky, and the dark outline of one great rock. His puzzled eyes came back to that rock even as the Mimi screamed again.

'The Nargun of the cave! It comes!'

'Back!' shouted Wirrun. 'Percy, get them back! Sam—Waratah—over this way!' He leapt backward away from the fires and had the men staring after him when the monster plunged. Then they leapt quickly enough.

The Nargun from the cave laid its terrible cry over the sea, 'Nga-a-a!' No one heard the Eldest on its boulder scream in reply like a tide-drawn pebble on a beach. The other plunged from the hill to the path and rolled and tumbled down, scrambling and pushing with squat invisible limbs. It passed above old Johnny crouching back against the hill, and thundered on scattering a wreckage of dead fires. From there they could not see how it went between rocks and pools and channels, only that it came on fast rumbling and grinding down the shelf. But they saw a darkness of empty eyes and a glimpse of snarling muzzle, and they watched, not breathing.

It did not turn towards the men but rumbled down the edge of the shelf beyond the fires; in among rocks, knocking some aside and smashing ice; out through the fires, scattering them; to rest at last between its most ancient brother and the sea. There was a long stillness on the shelf. The world itself hung still. At last the sea spoke one long peaceful word.

Even then the men did not speak; but they looked at each other, knowing what they had seen. No one moved towards the broken fires. They would go no closer; they did not even see that the broken ice was melting or that the rocks were stained white with the blood of Ninya.

The Ninya who were left were huddled in deep cracks at the edge of the shelf. 'We have lost six men,' said their leader bleakly. 'We must find another plan. We have not the strength for this one.'

The Nyols had crept away to the forest to see if the rocks were yet safe. The Dulugar had flown when the Nargun plunged; the Bagini's cockatoo-laugh came from inshore. They had left the mighty and ancient one, the First of Narguns, to the care of its brother. The men, finding they could breathe again, went up the shelf to see that old Johnny Wuthergul was safe. They found him unhurt, standing straight and gazing down the shelf.

'It'll be all right now,' said Johnny.

In the thunder of the Nargun's attack they had not heard the rattle-bang of an old car approaching. It was only when Wirrun saw himself coming from the wood-heap with three or four men and was shaking off the shock of this that he realized the men of Mount Conner had come. Relief and gladness rushed into him and he ran to meet them. The Yabon, taken by surprise but always helpful, slipped away behind the wood-heap and came back as a dog.

'Am I glad to see you!' cried Wirrun, holding out his hand.

They were surprised, for they thought he had been seeing them since he stopped them on the road last night; but they were glad to be greeted so warmly and shook hands again all round. Wirrun introduced them to the People of the settlement and told them quickly what had been happening and where he believed the Ninya were.

'They won't cause no more trouble,' said the oldest of the Mount Conner men comfortably. 'We come to sing them home.'

'Sooner you than me,' said Wirrun. 'It's a long way to sing.'

The men laughed, and the oldest explained kindly. 'We don't sing 'em the whole way. We sing 'em a little bit and wait along the way and sing a bit more. They'll go. There's others waiting up north'll sing 'em along. We split, see, account of cutting the road in half. We come south and they went north.' Wirrun admired the wisdom of this pincer movement, and the man shifted his eyes and spoke again with apology. 'When we get 'em home we won't let 'em out again.'

'Only I reckon you better hurry,' said Wirrun. 'The way they are, they might scatter again and we won't know where to find 'em. You want us to go?'

The men of Mount Conner shook their heads, for the song was not very big business. They were shown where the Narguns lay and went off down the shelf. The men of the settlement, their own part done, stayed under the hill to light one more fire and cook what breakfast they could for everyone.

Wirrun sat wearily down and patted the dog. He lay back on the warm sandy rock and listened to the sea. Above, where rock jutted from the hillside, he could see the Mimi; she was watching the Mount Conner men with brooding eyes. He wondered with a pang how she would enjoy travelling with them. Under the sound of the sea came the deep drone of chanting: a low strong song, rising gradually, breaking off and starting again.

Someone handed Wirrun a sausage folded in toast, and he ate it while he listened to the men of Mount Conner singing the Ninya home. And suddenly he slept.

He woke several hours later in the shade of the hill, with his pack beside him and a folded blanket under his head. There was no one else on the shelf; he was alone. Only the dog lay near, and over his head the Mimi perched. She was eating a root that she had roasted in dying coals, and a handful of ripe pigfaces lay beside her.

Wirrun sat up. 'Where have they gone?' he asked, bewildered.

The Mimi answered. 'Those of this country have left in their cars and would not let the others wake you. They have called you their brother and placed a gift under your head.'

Wirrun lowered his brows and gazed down the shelf. The tide had risen and was falling again, leaving a dark line of charcoal and charred wood. The Nargun of the cave lay sea-washed where it had rested, but Wirrun could not see its ancient brother. Back under the hill lay the four great mounds of ash that they had fed last night; the rock was grey and flaked around them, and Wirrun knew there would still be red coals deep inside. He fingered the blanket that the men had left. How they had worked; and he was too tired and drained to go after them. But he would come back. . . .

'Have the others gone too?' he asked, suddenly anxious for the Mimi.

'They have gone to their car near the stream; they have food there. They wait to take you home.'

'So we'll be travelling together a while longer yet,' said Wirrun, pleased; and then he saw that the Mimi was wearing her obstinate look.

'I go my own way,' she said.

'Come off it, Mimi, none of that. I'm too tired. The Ninya are going home through the rocks. They'll have their wind and their freezing, like before.'

'They go through caverns and I through rock. I will find a way.'

'You said you couldn't. You said that in strange rocks there were other spirits and they'd fight you.'

'Have I not ridden the winds and done all things that a Mimi cannot do? And should I ride home with men in a car like—'

'Like a can of peaches on wheels? No.' He never had managed to move the Mimi when she wore her obstinate look. He unfastened the power and held it up to her. 'You'll take this to watch out for you.' When she drew back he added, exasperated, 'You've used it before, and if anyone's earned the right you have. You could go on the wind.'

She would not touch the power. 'That is magic for the People,' she said, 'not for an earth-spirit. I will find my own way to my far dear land.'

Wirrun frowned in thought. Time was passing, the men might soon come, and he could not let the Mimi make that long journey without help. He put his hand on the black dog and said, 'Yabon. Do you want to help?'

If a man hears a dog talk he will turn into stone. The Yabon became a boy of the People.

'There is no spirit in this land,' said the boy, 'who would not help Wirrun the fighter of ice.'

'Right,' said Wirrun. '*Right!* Can you pass a message to all the rock-spirits? Get it sent along all the way through the land?'

'This message, I can,' said the Yabon. 'There are evil spirits as well as good, and countries that are hard to pass, but this message will fly through the land like a bird. For I will add whatever threats are needed and others will bear me out.'

'Good. Tell 'em a Mimi comes through to the north and all roads are open to her. Say that this Mimi's a Great One, she fought the ice all through the land.' He saw the Mimi's look of astonished pride and began to enlarge; she had earned whatever he or the spirits could give. 'Tell 'em to light her way with fires and see she has roots and lizards and rats. Wherever she goes she's free, whatever she wants they give, because she's the one that saved 'em from the ice. Tell 'em that.'

The Yabon rose, bowed to the delighted Mimi, walked a few steps up the path, and disappeared.

'Give him a bit of time,' said Wirrun to the Mimi, for he did not want to part from her too quickly. 'He won't be much past Tilba-Tilba yet.' The thought of Tilba-Tilba was a sadness added to the sadness of parting; for there lay the small frozen fighters, the only victims of the Ninya.

The Mimi was sitting very erect on her rock. 'You have shamed me,' she said proudly, 'for only you are the fighter. I am no fighter but—'

'A poor frail hider,' said Wirrun. 'I know. . . . I saw you looking at that Eldest Nargun. Tell me what you saw.'

'The Ancient One, the First, that we had come far to find.'

'Yeah. The mighty Eldest Nargun. Big as my hand.'

She hissed at him. 'A man! What does a man know of size? Greater than you is great, smaller than you is small; you know no more. There lies the Nargun from the cave: is it great? I tell you it lies among the stars smaller than a grain of sand.'

'H'm,' said Wirrun. 'Maybe. Only it wouldn't lie in a rockpool, would it?'

'And is not the rockpool a world among the stars? Life and death are in it, and light and darkness; there are journeys and home-coming there. Is a starfish smaller than a star?'

Wirrun was silent, hearing his own voice speaking to Ko-in: *There's a dung-beetle by that log. I care for that. There's a rotten toadstool with a worm in it: I care for both of 'em;* and Ko-in had answered: *You are of the People.* He must be tired if it took a Mimi to tell him what the People knew.

'Sometimes,' he said, teasing, 'I think I'd like you better if you weren't always right.' He stood up. 'But I want to remember you saying that, so don't say any more. I want it to be the last word. Till next time we meet any rate.' He knew the bit about next time was a lie, but the lie was spoken to cushion the truth that must come. 'Goodbye, Mimi. I won't forget you. And thanks.'

He bowed as the Yabon had done, and she bowed back with dark sad eyes like a possum's, and he took up his pack once more and walked away.

Nothing plucked at the loop of fur-cord that hung from his belt. He walked up the inlet to a shabby waiting car and the men from Mount Conner.

Glossary

Abo—Aborigine of Australia; familiar form of reference.

Bagini—inimical spirit; looks like a girl of the People, but with dangerous claws on her fingers.

banksia—a shrub or tree, bearing dense yellow flowers.

Bunyip—dreaded monster spirit of great power; dwells in shallow water to trap and kill men for food.

corroboree—a large, noisy gathering or festival of the People.

currawong—a bird of prey.

Dulugar—a hairy, dark manlike spirit that attacks women.

Eldest Nargun, the—an ancient, living rock with the power of fire; defeated the Ninya long ago and routed the Ice Age.

firestick—a torch of wood.

gum (tree)—eucalyptus tree.

Happy Folk—the whites of Australia who continue a life like that of Europeans; especially, the city dwellers.

Holden—a make of automobile.

Inlanders—whites who have lived close to the land long enough to have developed some feeling for it.

Mimi—shy spirits who live inside rocks; very tall, thin, and frail.

Mrart—spirit of a dead person.

mulga—a slow-growing type of tree.

mulgara—a small predator.

Nargun—creatures of living rock; considered Great Powers.

Net-Net—small, hairy, gray spirits who live among, but not in, rocks.

Ninya—ice-spirits, manlike but formed of ice; makers of ice, living in underground ice caverns.

nulla-nulla—a hardwood club, sometimes sharpened at the end.

Nyols—little spirit-People who live within rocks.

People, the—the black Aborigines of Australia.

spinifex—spiny grass.

Thian-Malkia—spirits who weave nets to trap prey.

walkabout—wandering across country.

Wa-tha-gun-darl—little, tough spirit-people who live in caves and shun fire.

Yabon—shape-changing, friendly spirit; capable of being seen by the People.

Yauruks—great, white spirit-birds who hunt whales for the People.

NOTE: The spirits of the Australian People bear little resemblance to the pale, ghostly things of European mythology. The spirits of the People's legends are normally invisible but otherwise have many of the characteristics of life. They work or seek prey to eat, they suffer pain and emotional reactions, and they have a real existence and physical ability. They are also frequently limited in territory. They do not spring from the People, but from the land, and many are older than mankind in the land.

Enchanting fantasies from